'You're the only person I've ever employed who answers me back.'

'And is that why I'm still here?' Claris asked.

'Probably.' Returning his attention to the baby, Adam handed him a plastic shape which promptly went into his mouth. 'I don't know if he's hungry or just teething.'

'Both, I expect. It's time for his lunch anyway.'

He shouldn't have kissed her, he thought as he watched her unpack the baby's lunch. It had made her wary, and that wasn't what he wanted at all. Not that he was entirely sure *what* he wanted. He only knew that the delightful Miss Newman was seriously disrupting the calm waters of his normally agreeable existence. A new experience for him. As was the baby. They had both given him thoughts he didn't normally have.

Emma Richmond was born during the war in North Kent when, she says, 'farms were the norm and motorways non-existent. My childhood was one of warmth and adventure. Amiable and disorganised, I'm married with three daughters, all of whom have fled the nest—probably out of exasperation! The dog stayed, reluctantly. I'm an avid reader, a compulsive writer and a besotted new granny. I love life and my world of dreams, and all I need to make things complete is a housekeeper—like, yesterday!'

Recent titles by the same author:

BRIDEGROOM ON LOAN
THE RELUCTANT GROOM

THE
BOSS'S BRIDE

BY
EMMA RICHMOND

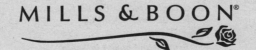

First published in Great Britain 1999
Harlequin Mills & Boon Limited,
Eton House, 18-24 Paradise Road, Richmond, Surrey TW9 1SR

© Emma Richmond 1999

ISBN 0 263 81846 2

Set in Times Roman 10½ on 12¼ pt.
02-9911-43760 C1

Printed and bound in Spain
by Litografia Rosés, S.A., Barcelona

PROLOGUE

WITH an air of profound boredom, Adam Turmaine wandered over to an old print hanging above the hall table. Extending one finger, he touched it to the bottom right-hand corner. 'What does that say?'

Claris leaned closer and informed him drily, 'Treasury of Mechanical Music.'

'Most appalling writing I've ever seen in my life. What am I doing here?'

'Waiting to meet your aunt.'

Removing his gaze from the ancient map of Rye, he gave his companion a long look of contemplation. 'Do I have an aunt?'

Claris's lip twitched.

'I'll take that as an affirmative, although why you would think I'd be even remotely interested in meeting a distant relative, I can't imagine.'

'Because she's family?' she guessed. 'Because there have been anonymous phone calls hinting that her financial advisor is ripping her off?'

'What a singularly disgusting expression, and you really must stop trying to fit me with this mantle of concern for other people's affairs,' he drawled as he returned his attention to the map. 'How long have you worked for me?'

'You know how long I've worked for you.'

'Then you should know by now that I'm not in the

least family-minded.' Turning, he gave her a warm smile. 'You'd better point her out to me.'

'Adam! You must know what your aunt looks like!'

'Must I? Why?'

Eyes full of amusement, she merely looked at him.

'It's been *years*, Claris,' he excused himself. 'The last time I saw her was at my uncle's funeral.' Glancing into the reception room behind her, he encountered several pairs of eyes all looking at him. They smiled in disconcerting unison. He didn't smile back. 'Who *are* all these people?'

'Local dignitaries, I think. It's only natural they would want to meet you.'

'Is it? Have I ever evinced an interest in meeting a complete stranger?'

'No,' she denied drily.

'Then I can't imagine why they should. We only arrived a few days ago, and already I'm expected to visit...'

'Colonel Davenport,' Claris put in helpfully.

'Colonel Davenport,' he agreed. 'A man I do not know, have never to my knowledge met, and whom I have no desire to meet, but who seems to think it imperative I concern myself with local vandalism.'

'That's because he doesn't know you,' she murmured, tongue in cheek.

'But you do,' he informed her softly, 'which makes it all the more amazing that you seem to expect me to concern myself in my aunt's affairs. And what colossal cheek on my part it would be to assume that she's incapable of looking after her own investments.'

Halting, he suddenly gave a small frown. 'On the other hand...'

Claris waited.

'My memory of her, which I would be the first to admit can sometimes be faulty—'

'Selective,' Claris put in.

'—is of a fluttery woman who couldn't string two sentences together.'

'I expect you made her nervous.'

He looked genuinely astonished. 'Why on earth would I make her nervous?'

Claris gave a wry smile. 'Do you have any other relatives?'

He pulled a face. 'What a sobering thought. I had hoped I didn't have *any*.'

'You don't mean that...'

'I don't?' Adam asked in surprise.

'No. So now come and meet her. You can't stand out in the hall all evening—' Breaking off, because she knew her employer could do just that if he had a mind to, she added, 'Please?'

Adam sighed. 'Very well, but I do wish you would curb this enthusiasm you have for pitching me into situations I have no desire for.'

'*I* pitch you? You were the one who accepted the invitation.'

'I didn't understand the details—oh, God, who's this?'

Turning quickly, Claris stared at a very large lady in puce who was emerging from the rear of the hall. The woman halted, beamed, and then held out both hands as though greeting a long-lost friend. 'Mr Turmaine!'

Adam deftly avoided an embrace.

'I had no idea you'd arrived!'

And someone's head was going to roll, Claris thought in amusement, for that little oversight.

'I'm your hostess. Mrs Staple Smythe.'

Claris could see a rude comment coming, so she kicked Adam's ankle. Hard.

He grunted something.

'And is this your wife?'

'I don't have a wife,' he denied coldly.

'Oh. Only we assumed…'

'Yes?' he queried hatefully.

'Nothing, it's not important,' she denied hastily. 'But please don't stand out here being shy. Come and meet everyone.' She gave Claris a look of query, and when neither of them enlightened her she gave another awkward smile and turned to go into the room.

'Shy?' Adam queried, *sotto voce*.

She gave a little choke of laughter and urged him in their hostess's wake.

'Your aunt Harriet is here,' she continued, 'and longing to meet you again. She's such a dear friend…'

'Is she?' he enquired, in a tone of voice that made it quite clear that he found such a friendship totally incomprehensible.

Slightly unnerved, she halted. 'Let me get you both a drink.'

It was left to Claris to thank her. 'It wouldn't hurt you to be *nice*,' she reproved Adam.

'Yes, it would. She's the sort of woman I most dislike.' Scanning the crowded room, he finally pronounced, 'I think my aunt's the one in grey.'

'Then go and talk to her.'

'And then we can go home?' he asked hopefully.

She merely smiled, knowing very well that he would go home when he wanted, exactly when he wanted, with no care as to whom he offended.

He took his drink from his hostess's hand, and before she could launch into further conversation walked away.

'He's gone to talk to his aunt,' Claris explained mildly.

'Then he's heading in the wrong direction,' she said waspishly.

Claris gave another little choke of laughter. 'It's a long time since he's seen her.'

Handing Claris her drink—a rather watery-looking white wine—she said almost petulantly, 'I don't know who you are.'

Claris felt momentarily sorry for her hostess, who had obviously had such high hopes of Adam Turmaine, but Adam behaved as he wanted to behave, with no thought for anyone's feelings but his own. She wondered if she ought to warn her. 'I'm Claris Newman,' she explained, really rather unhelpfully, she knew, but her boss did so abhor anyone knowing his business. And that included the role his assistant played in his life.

Before Claris could even attempt to minimise the hostility her hostess was obviously feeling, she broke in hurriedly, 'Will you excuse me? I naturally need to circulate.'

'Of course.' With an amused light in her eyes at her dismissal, Claris watched Mrs Staple Smythe forge a way to Adam's side. Foolish woman. She was only going to open herself up to more snubs. Adam hated pretension. But then, Adam hated a lot of things, especially parties, which made it all the more amazing that he had actually volunteered to come to this one.

Carefully moving to a nearby corner, where she would be out of the way, she watched her employer. He was a tall, slim man, with a languid elegance. Working for him was better than watching a play. A townie at heart, Claris hadn't been sure she was going to like living in the country, and after meeting these people tonight she was even *less* sure. On the other hand, if she hadn't come with him to this small village near Rye she would have had to leave him, and she really didn't want to work for anyone else. Which, on the face of it, seemed crazy. Spoilt by reason of his vast wealth, he was selfish, and mocking, but he set her challenges that no other employer ever had. He also set her heart beating erratically, she thought sadly, and that, quite simply, couldn't be allowed. *Wouldn't* be allowed.

With a rather self-mocking twist to her mouth, she moved her gaze to the others in the room. She thought they looked a self-important lot. Not that she would probably have much to do with them.

Various people came up, introduced themselves, asked her questions, which she evaded, and then, thankfully, she was left alone—so that they could talk about her. She wasn't being paranoid; she could tell by the sidelong glances she kept receiving that she was being discussed. She felt amused rather than alarmed, and dismissed the matter from her mind.

Adam was now talking to a woman in blue—hopefully the aunt. A young slender woman with dark hair stood beside them, staring at Adam as though he was the answer to all her prayers. Perhaps he was. The woman in blue broke away, and headed towards Claris.

Here came the inquisition. There was always an inquisition. On the rare occasions she accompanied Adam to a function, usually to pick someone's brains for him, interrogation had always been part of the evening. Almost paranoid about his privacy, Adam deliberately never explained their relationship, and people found it hard to understand how such a good-looking, successful man could have such a drab for his escort. Lips twitching into a smile at her analogy, she stared down into her drink. She wasn't a drab, but then neither was she a great beauty. Her copper hair tended towards ginger rather than beech trees, her fair skin was freckled, and her wide grey eyes held amusement rather than mystery. But she was clever. Which was why Adam employed her.

'And you are?' a haughty voice enquired, and Claris looked up quickly. The woman in blue stood in front of her. She was a handsome woman, a little on the thin side, perhaps, but elegant. Certainly not the nervous babbler that Adam had remembered. If indeed this was his aunt.

'Claris Newman,' she introduced herself. 'Are you Mrs Turmaine?'

'Yes. How well do you know him?' she demanded bluntly.

'Well enough.'

'Is he permanently fixed down here?'

'Why don't you ask him?'

'I did. He said to ask you.'

Claris merely looked at her.

'Hmph. What's this I hear about a baby?'

'I don't know,' she denied. 'What is it that you hear?'

A look of aggravation crossed her face. 'You were seen arriving with one.'

'Was I?'

'Yes. Is it his? Are you sleeping with him?'

'Are you always this rude?' Claris countered.

'In love with him?'

'None of your business,' she reproved, without inflexion.

Turning, Mrs Turmaine stared across the room at her nephew. 'Time he was married and settled down. Good-looking men who play the field are usually bad news.'

Were they? To whom? Claris wondered. After sipping her drink, which was awful, she wedged it onto the crowded table beside her. Moving her eyes back to Adam, she considered his aunt's statement. Yes, he was good-looking—no, she mentally denied, the man was devastating, but not necessarily bad news. He could sometimes be very rude. Must run in the family. His aunt was even ruder. He could also be aggravating, kind, and thoughtful. He also had a great deal of charm. When he cared to use it. His dark hair was thick, with a slight curl, his brown eyes direct. He was clever and challenging, and generous when he wanted to be. And, no, she wasn't in love with him. She was attracted to him, she admitted, and it was an attraction she fought every minute of every day, but she was not in love. Any more than he was in love with her. The thought that it might even be conceivable brought a warped smile to her face. She wasn't even sure that he was capable of loving. He was fond of his godson, which was the only reason he had moved to the house outside Rye—so that he could care for him whilst his parents were in hospital recovering from a horrendous car crash. His London apartment was totally unsuitable for a baby; the baby's home was in Norfolk, and too far for easy access to the hospital, so they had come to the house he owned in the village of Wentsham. Little Nathan was probably the nearest he'd ever come to loving another human being. By his own admission he had no desire to marry, have children of his own...

'What does he do?'

Wrenching her attention back to his aunt, Claris asked with deliberate vagueness, 'Do?'

'Yes, *do*. It surely can't be a secret!'

'No-o,' she denied, 'but I would prefer that you ask him yourself.'

'I know he owns property,' Harriet said crossly, as though it was some sort of sin.

'Yes.'

'And an electronics firm.'

'Yes.'

'And land. He's extremely wealthy.'

'Is he?' asked Claris, who knew almost down to the last penny how much he was worth.

With eyes as direct as her nephew's, Harriet Turmaine stared at Claris for some moments in silence. 'It's none of my business what he does, but I'll give you a word of warning. This is a small community—old-fashioned, some might say—but if the baby's yours, and he's the father, and if he's intending to stay here, he'd do better to marry you. I shan't live in his pocket,' she promised bluntly. 'It's not my way. No need to worry that I'll interfere. Couldn't if I wanted to. Don't like people much.' With an abrupt nod, she walked away.

Interesting, Claris thought. Related to Adam by marriage, not blood, astonishingly, she seemed very much like him. With a small smile, Claris made her way towards her employer, who was looking bored. She raised her eyebrows at him and amusement leached into his eyes.

'Bored, Claris?' he asked naughtily.

She gave him a look of mild derision and removed the glass from his hand. 'Say goodbye to your hostess,' she instructed him.

His amusement deeper, he went to do so.

'Always does as he's told, does he?' a soft voice asked from beside her, and she turned to look at the young woman who had been talking to him.

'Not always, no,' she denied pleasantly. 'It was nice to have met you,' she added, by way of dismissal.

'But you haven't.'

'No,' Claris agreed.

'I'm Bernice Long. Harriet's niece. Her sister's daughter. I expect we'll meet again.'

It sounded like a warning. 'Yes. Goodnight.' A small smile on her mouth, she made her way towards their hostess, who had one hand resting rather intimately on Adam's sleeve.

'Thank you for a pleasant evening,' Claris murmured, and Mrs Staple Smythe turned with a look of irritation.

'I'm sure I don't know why you have to leave so soon. You've only just arrived.'

'Yes, but we don't like to leave the baby too long.' As an exit line, it was as good as any. With a last smile, she walked out. She wanted very badly to laugh.

'A ghastly evening,' Adam commented as they stepped outside.

'Yes. I don't think we endeared ourselves.'

'Were we meant to?' he drawled.

She laughed. 'And if that is a sample of Rye hospitality...'

'It isn't, and this isn't Rye. It's a small village. Probably inbred,' he commented indifferently as he headed towards the gate.

'Well, you would know. You were born here.'

'But I haven't lived here since the age of eight. And eight-year-olds, my dear Miss Newman, aren't known for their perspicacity.'

'No,' she agreed as she walked with him along the narrow lane. The well-manicured, immaculately hedged lane. Twenty or so detached houses and a small general store seemed the sum total of the community. Adam's house was the last one on the right-hand side. Not that it could be seen behind its high brick wall, but that was where it was, and where she would be living for the next few months.

They walked in silence for a few moments, and then she asked curiously, 'What was she like?'

'Who?'

'Bernice Long. The young woman you were talking to.'

'I wasn't aware I was talking to anyone.'

In other words, Claris thought wryly, mind your own business. 'What did you think of your aunt?'

'I don't think I thought anything,' he denied. 'Why the remark about the baby?' he asked, in the sort of voice that had often reduced past secretaries to tears. He'd had a great many secretaries, or so she'd been told. None of them had lasted very long.

'I was being naughty,' she said simply.

'Then I would appreciate it if you would learn to contain it, and not make injudicious remarks.'

'It wasn't injudicious,' she denied, without offence. 'Your aunt had already asked me about it.'

'And you told her?'

She slanted him a glance of derision.

'Sorry,' he apologised.

'Accepted. She said she didn't intend to live in your pocket.'

'I'm very glad to hear it.'

'But I suspect the same couldn't be said of Mrs Staple Smythe.'

'Then you had best make sure my pockets are always unavailable, hadn't you? And don't sigh.' With one of his quicksilver changes of moods, he promised humorously, 'I'll let you look after the baby tomorrow.'

'How kind. Sadly, I will be unable to take you up on your generous offer. If you want your printer replaced, I shall have to go to London and bully someone.'

'Bully them over the phone.'

'But it works so much better face-to-face,' she informed him softly as she pushed open the narrow side gate that led into the extensive grounds. 'Anyway, I have to see the letting agent about my flat.' She thought it might also be wise to try and change the sub-lease from long-term to short. In case she needed a bolt-hole. Having met the residents, she wasn't entirely sure she was going to like living in Wentsham.

CHAPTER ONE

THE Secret Garden, Claris thought humorously as she all but circumnavigated the red-brick wall before finding the rear entrance. Pushing open the gate, she stepped quietly inside. Enchanted, she halted to stare about her. Trees, shrubs, ancient statuary, and a flowering vine that scrambled unchecked over an old pergola. Closing her eyes, she breathed in the heady scent of honeysuckle. The sun was warm on her face, and for the first time in days she felt at peace. She hadn't even known this part of the garden existed, but then, she thought wryly, the last few hectic days hadn't given her much time for investigation.

Looking after Adam's business interests was a difficult enough job. Adding a fourteen-month-old baby to the equation made it almost impossible. Before moving to Wentsham, she had wondered how hard would it be. Hard, was the answer. She had sort of assumed that a one-year-old would sit quietly and play with his toys—when he wasn't asleep, that was. Not true. Nathan was *active*. So was Adam. Apart from helping out with the baby, he had expected her to set up his office in the house so that everything ran smoothly to beg, plead, sob, in order to get another phone line put in *immediately*, and then, hastily and exhaustingly, remove everything from the baby's path. A one-baby demolition derby, that was what Nathan was. She must have run *miles* just chasing after him to prevent an accident. Not that she'd had to do it *all* herself. Adam was *trying* to be practical. He was also desperately worried about his friends, Nathan's parents. Paul was still in a coma, Jenny in and out of consciousness but seemingly unaware of what had happened. Jenny's parents, who had been in the car with them, weren't on the critical list, but it would be weeks before they could be discharged. Which left only Adam, and herself, and his house-keeper to look after the baby.

Reluctant to move on, Claris spent another few mo-ments just listening to the gentle buzzing of the bees in the honeysuckle, the call of a lone blackbird, and then began following the narrow, meandering path to-wards the small gate she could see ahead of her. Opening it, she stepped through into the garden proper. The manicured lawn, courtesy of an excellent gardener, looked almost emerald after the morning's rain. A riotous profusion of flowers bordered each side, spilling lazily across the paths, and led the eye towards the old red-brick house before her. Grays Manor. Envy was as foreign to her nature as greed, but this house generated it in her. The first time she had seen it she had wanted it to be hers. Dream on.

With a wry smile she began walking along the path, past the French doors that stood slightly open, until she came to another wrought-iron gate. Pushing it open, she entered the paved courtyard. A vintage car stood before the old stable block. A pair of long legs protruded horizontally from the left-hand side—and the baby was crawling determinedly towards a cat that was lazily sunning itself beside a tub of geraniums.

'Hello, pumpkin,' she greeted softly, and the baby

presumably knowing he was about to be thwarted, increased his pace towards his goal. With a laugh in her eyes, she walked across to the car and gently touched her foot to one protruding leg. And no one would ever know, she thought pensively, how such a small action could set her heart beating into over-drive. With no hint of how she was feeling in her voice, she asked quietly, 'Should that baby be crawl-ing out here unattended?'

There was the thump of a head hitting the bottom of the car, a curse, and then the rapid emergence of the mechanic. Dark tousled hair, a filthy face, hands covered in black grease, one of which held a spanner. Dark eyes surveyed her with languid interest before he turned his head to watch the baby.

'He's investigating,' Adam drawled. 'He won't come to any harm. Lydia's watching him, and you're late.'

'Traffic was bad,' she said mildly. Checking to see that the housekeeper really was watching him, she walked on. Some days were better than others. Some days she could get through all their working hours without actually wanting to touch him. And some days she couldn't. With a determination she some-times found quite frightening, she firmly dismissed the matter.

Reaching the side door of the house, which stood open, she walked quietly inside. A feeling of age en-veloped her, of centuries past, and she breathed in the heady aroma of polish and musk and antiquity. A baby-gate was fixed incongruously across the bottom of the beautiful staircase.

'I love this house,' she murmured.

'You can't afford it,' Adam said from behind her.

'Yet,' she said softly, and he laughed.

Turning, she watched him wiping his hands on an oily rag. She wasn't quite sure which was doing the best job of transferring the grease. 'I forgot to take the device to open the front gates,' she informed him, 'and so I had to leave my car in the lane and walk round the back.'

He grunted.

'But if I hadn't done that, I wouldn't have found the secret garden. It's beautiful.'

'It's a mess.'

She smiled again. 'You have no soul.' Her heels clipped on the tiled floor as she walked into the room on the left, and then she halted. Boxes littered the floor; files were stacked on the desk, the chair, and on one of the filing cabinets. Paper spewed from the fax machine and the computer was buried beneath the pink sheets of the *Financial Times*. Turning, she gave Adam a look of admonishment.

'Neville sent down the rest of the papers I needed,' he told her indolently as he leaned in the doorway. 'I'll clear them away later.'

'Your accountant knows very well that the information is on disk,' she countered mildly. 'We don't *need* paper.'

'I do. What did they say?'

'Two weeks.'

He waited, eyes amused.

She gave a slow smile. 'You know me too well.' In fact, he didn't know her at all. There was a clunk from behind him, and they both turned to look. With a little tsk, Adam bent down to remove the radiator cap from the baby's fist. 'No,' he said firmly.

Nathan beamed at him and crawled energetically towards Claris. Using her legs as an aid, little fingers pinching into the flesh, causing her to wince, he climbed to his feet and stared up at her. His scrutiny was as intense as hers. And then he laughed and tugged on her skirt. Dropping her large handbag, she bent to scoop him up and into her arms, and then gave a little grunt of pain as he dug his feet into her waist and proceeded to try and climb higher. All attempts at restraint failed.

'You're a pickle,' she told him. 'And don't pull my hair.'

'Dib, dib.'

She grinned, and he suddenly lunged forward, mouth open to reveal a row of tiny teeth. Quickly jerking backwards, she gently placed him back on the floor. 'Piranha,' she scolded.

'How well *do* I know you?' he prompted.

'Well enough to know that your replacement printer will be here tomorrow.'

'And if it wasn't?' he asked softly.

'Then the order would be cancelled and we would go somewhere else.' There was a slithering sound and she turned quickly to see the pile of files on the chair slowly topple.

Adam was faster, and scooped the baby out of the way of the avalanche just in time. She took Nathan from him before he could get grease all over the baby, and put him down the other side of the desk. Like a needle to a magnet, he headed straight for the bookcase.

'And?'

'And I would make very sure that their reputation suffered,' she added as she headed in the same direction. 'I'm a very good—negotiator.' The bookcase wasn't fixed to the wall, and she held it steady as the baby hauled himself upright and put one foot on the bottom shelf—from where the books had all been removed. Yesterday. In haste. 'Did you really expect me to fail?'

'No. You're a very resourceful lady.'

'Clever,' she corrected with a grin. 'The word is "clever". No,' she added softly.

Nathan looked at her, looked at the bookcase, thumped to his bottom and went to investigate the wastepaper basket instead.

'We'll have to—' she began.

'We?'

Pursing her lips, eyes alight with self-mockery, she corrected, 'I will have to get someone to screw it to the wall. I called in at the hospital,' she added quietly. 'No change. I said you'd be in later.'

He nodded.

Her eyes on the baby, she said, 'He's adjusted very well, hasn't he? It's only when he wakes up... It breaks my heart,' she added softly, 'to see the look of expectancy on his face, as though this time it will be his mother, but then he smiles... He's such a *happy* baby.'

'I thought you didn't like babies?' he mocked softly.

'I didn't say I didn't *like* them; I said I didn't know anything about them. Has he had his lunch?'

He nodded again.

'Then I'll take him up for his nap.' Scooping up the baby, she walked out. Hitching up her skirt, she climbed over the baby-gate and walked slowly upstairs. And, almost against her will, the feel of the warm, squirmy body in her arms woke something inside that she thought would never again entirely sleep. She'd never had very much to do with babies, and would have said, even as little as a week ago, that she wasn't maternal. And yet this energetic little scrap was beginning to tug on her heartstrings as no one else ever had.

Gently stroking his hair, she walked into his bedroom and laid him in his cot. 'Go to sleep,' she ordered softly as she bent to give him a kiss. Putting a light blanket over him, she smiled into the big blue eyes staring up at her. He was beautiful, and appealing, and he made her want to smile. Even Adam wasn't immune, though he tried to pretend he was.

Walking across to the window, she drew the curtains. Picking up the baby alarm, she went quietly out. Back in her own room, she changed out of her suit into a loose skirt and top, shoved her feet into flat, comfy sandals, clipped the alarm to her belt, and went down to the kitchen to beg a cup of coffee from Lydia.

The housekeeper wasn't a great one for chatting, but then neither was Claris. Accepting her coffee with a smile, she walked back to the study. Adam still stood in the centre of the floor, wiping his hands, a look of distraction on his strong face. And the phone was ringing.

Picking up the receiver, she listened, nodded, then agreed quietly, 'That will be fine.' Replacing the phone, she scribbled a note in the diary and then glanced at her employer. He had moved to stare through the door into the side garden. 'Mackenzie will come and see you about the land on Friday afternoon,' she told him.

He gave an absent nod and began to walk out, no doubt to continue tinkering with his old car. The old car that was entered in the endurance rally to be held the following month. The rally he would now have to miss.

Seconds later he was back.

'That woman's out there,' he informed her, almost accusingly.

Her lips twitched. 'Which woman?'

'Puce.'

'Puce?' she asked in bewilderment as he headed towards the hall, and then realised who he meant. 'Oh.'

'I'm going to have a shower.'

'Adam,' she warned.

Ignoring her, he continued out, and she heard his soft footsteps as he ascended the stairs.

Moments later Lydia appeared, to tell her that a Mrs Staple Smythe was here.

With yet another invitation? Claris wondered. Tempted to tell Lydia to get rid of her, she opened her mouth to do so, and then changed her mind. Perhaps she ought to see her, try and get things onto a warmer footing. Alienating neighbours was never a good plan. 'Show her into the lounge, would you, Lydia?' she asked resignedly.

'Tea? Best china?'

'I'm tempted to tell you to use chipped mugs, if we had any, which I don't suppose we do…'

'I'm sure I could manufacture some,' Lydia proposed helpfully.

Laughing, Claris shook her head. 'No, but use the smallest cups you can find. I feel I ought to see her, but I don't want a *prolonged* visit.' Upsetting Mrs Staple Smythe wouldn't achieve anything, might even do untold harm, and this was why Adam paid her so well, after all: to deal with the minor, and sometimes major irritations in his life. Mrs Staple Smythe, she thought gloomily, was definitely one of the latter ones. But she had clout, Claris had discovered, and if Adam's life was to run smoothly then the Mrs Staple Smythes of this world couldn't be entirely ignored. Unfortunately.

Walking across the hall, she observed the other woman unseen for a moment. She looked as though she were mentally pricing every ornament and picture. The puce of last evening had been replaced by yellow. Pearl studs graced her ears, a pearl choker her neck. Rather overdressed for an afternoon visit.

Claris cleared her throat and walked into the room. 'Mrs Staple Smythe,' she greeted politely. 'How nice of you to call. Won't you sit down? The housekeeper will bring us some tea.'

'Thank you.'

When she was seated, Claris took the chair opposite.

'I thought I saw Mr Turmaine…?' Allowing the question to hang in the air, Mrs Staple Smythe waited.

'He's unavailable, I'm afraid. What can I do for you?'

'I don't imagine you can do anything for me, Miss Newman,' she said with a sweetness that grated. 'It was merely a social call.'

'I see.' And reproof that they hadn't sent a little note to thank her for her party? Deciding that offence was better than defence, Claris added, 'I was just about to pen you a thank-you note. As you can no doubt imagine, having only just moved in, everything has been at sixes and sevens, but there's really no excuse for my tardiness.'

'*Your* tardiness?' asked Mrs Staple Smythe pointedly, and then gave a silly little laugh. 'I get so confused with all these modern arrangements, people living together. "Partners" they call them now, don't they?'

'Do they?' Claris asked unhelpfully.

Not one whit discomfited, and clearly determined to find out all she could, Mrs Staple Smythe continued, 'Small towns are such a hotbed of gossip. You were seen arriving with the baby, and naturally everyone was—interested.'

'Naturally,' Claris agreed.

Glancing at the baby alarm still clipped to Claris's belt, she asked. 'He's yours?'

'His name's Nathan,' Claris answered naughtily, as though she'd misunderstood the question, 'and here comes Lydia with our tea.'

Smiling at the housekeeper, who could make a clam appear voluble, Claris asked her to put the tray on the small table. Lydia nodded and retreated.

'She isn't local,' Mrs Staple Smythe commented.

'No. Do you take milk and sugar?'

'Milk, no sugar. You come from London, do you?'

'Yes. How long have you lived here?'

'Oh, for ever,' she laughed.

'One of the leading lights?' Claris asked pleasantly.

'On the committee, of course. To deal with local matters. It is, of course, traditional for the owner of the Manor to show an interest in local affairs. Naturally, with Mr Turmaine living away, it would have been a little difficult for him to participate. But now that he's back…'

He'd be expected to, what? Sit on committees? Oh, boy. Wondering how to delicately phrase a warning that Adam was unlikely to do any such thing, Claris slowly poured the tea and handed it over. 'Does his aunt—participate?'

She looked astonished. 'Of course not. She lives in Rye,' she said, as though that adequately answered the question. Seeing Claris's puzzlement, she elaborated shortly, 'Wentsham is a separate entity. We have our own way of doing things. Only residents have any say in anything.'

And woe betide anyone who didn't do as they were told?

'I would really have preferred to explain all this to Mr Turmaine.'

'He's a very busy man,' Claris managed diplomatically.

'Perhaps if you could just tell him I'm here?' she prompted.

'It wouldn't do any good, I'm afraid. He left strict instructions not to be disturbed.'

With a sigh that sounded both disbelieving and cross, Mrs Staple Smythe opened her bag, removed a folded piece of paper and handed it across. 'Perhaps you would make sure he gets it. It's our summer schedule.'

'Thank you.'

'Harriet wasn't quite sure who you were,' she continued busily. 'What role you might play in her nephew's life.'

'Wasn't she?'

Thwarted, Mrs Staple Smythe ground her teeth. 'No,' she agreed. 'I'm not trying to be nosy...'

Yes, you are, Claris thought.

'...but it's a little difficult to know how to deal with you.' She smiled, as if to take the sting out of her words. 'You're his social secretary, perhaps? Act as his hostess?' The questions were asked with an air of disbelief, as though no one of Mrs Staple Smythe's standing could possibly understand a man of Adam's breeding associating with a—nobody. 'I don't believe I know of any Newmans. Your family home is where?'

Tempted to laugh outright at the feudality of it all, Claris bit her lip. 'My family home is in Leicester. And if you're about to ask me what my father did, or if my parents were married, please don't,' she added pleasantly. 'Don't let your tea get cold.'

'No.' Raising her cup, Mrs Staple Smythe slowly sipped—and tried again. 'We were all so excited when we heard Mr Turmaine was coming to take up residence amongst us. Such a shame to leave a beautiful old house like this in the hands of caretakers. Mr Turmaine was born here, I believe?'

'Yes,' Claris agreed, and knew very well that Mrs Staple Smythe had probably researched the whole family back to William the Conqueror. 'Did you know his father?'

'No,' she denied with obvious regret. 'And although you obviously think my concerns about who lives in the village very silly, if we don't find out what people do, what sort of background they have, there is a very real danger that the community will degenerate.'

'I understand perfectly, and I promise that I will try not to be the cause of any—degeneration. And now, I'm afraid, I really am very busy.' Standing, she waited for Mrs Staple Smythe to do the same. 'I'll make sure Mr Turmaine gets the schedule, but I'm afraid I can't promise that he will do anything about it. As I said earlier, his free time is rather limited. I'll see you out, shall I?'

With quite obvious reluctance, she followed Claris into the hall. 'It's a beautiful house,' she commented stiffly.

'Yes.'

'Very old, of course.'

'Yes. Thank you for calling, and for inviting us to meet everyone. Goodbye.'

With nowhere left to go but out, Mrs Staple Smythe rather ungraciously retreated. Claris thankfully closed the door on her.

'Very masterful,' Adam complimented from the top of the stairs.

Looking up, she gave him an unsmiling glance. 'I've been taking leaves out of your book. She brought your schedule.'

'I beg your pardon?'

'Your schedule.' Opening the piece of paper she

still held in her hand, she quickly glanced at it and then handed it across as he slowly descended the stairs. 'Dates of the committee meetings I imagine you are expected to attend.'

He crumpled it.

'I also imagine that Mrs Staple Smythe and her cronies will make life very difficult for you if you don't—comply.'

'Then you had best make sure they don't. Hadn't you?' he asked softly. Climbing over the baby-gate, he strolled towards the study. 'We have a meeting with a systems analyst Friday evening in Rye,' he tossed over his shoulder. 'I've booked a private room. His name's Mark Davies, wife Sara. He needs marketing and investment for an apparently revolutionary new system he's invented. It looks good on paper, but you know more about the technical side than I do. I left the file on your desk. Be ready at seven-thirty, will you? Did you ring Neville back?'

'No, I'll do it now.'

'He has no idea why the disks you sent him don't work,' he explained.

'Probably forgot to switch the computer on.'

He laughed. 'It surely couldn't be that simple.'

'Oh, it could. You wouldn't believe the idiocy of some people.'

'He isn't an idiot. Technology overtook him,' he added with gentle reproof. 'Megabytes to some people mean big teeth.'

With a wry smile, she agreed. 'OK, I'll be gentle with him.'

'You're always gentle.'

'No,' she denied softly. 'I'm not. Mrs Staple Smythe wanted to know if I was your partner.'

'What did you tell her?'

'That the baby's name was Nathan.'

He gave a delighted laugh. 'And I thought you such a mouse when I first met you.'

'Appearances can be deceptive,' she murmured, in a parody of his own drawl.

'I know,' he agreed. 'Oh, how I know. You must never leave me, Claris. Life would be incredibly flat without you.'

'It might be incredibly difficult with me,' she countered.

Giving her a sharp glance, his voice very soft, he asked, 'Meaning?'

'Meaning stupid women can sometimes be very dangerous. Mrs Staple Smythe is a snob of the worst kind. She expected you to have a suitable wife that she could manipulate.'

'Instead of which, she found you.'

'Yes. No background. She'd never heard of the Newmans,' she added with slight dryness. 'An unmarried mother...'

'I beg your pardon?'

'She assumes the baby is mine,' she explained. 'Which might have been forgiven if I'd had any semblance of style, and had answered her pertinent questions.'

'You want to tell her the truth?'

'No,' she denied. Not only because she knew how much Adam hated people to know his business, but because Mrs Staple Smythe had put her own back up, and she now didn't *want* her to know. 'But I'll bet

you anything you like to name that she will cause
trouble. One way or another, I'm going to be pun-
ished.'

She didn't know how right she was.

He didn't say anything for a while, merely watched
her, eyes slightly narrowed. 'If you can't deal with
it...'

'Did I say that?' she queried as she walked across
to her desk and switched on her computer.

'No.'

'But when your grass verges remain uncut, when
your access is repeatedly blocked...'

'I'm not sitting on any committees, Claris.'

'No,' she agreed. 'But I begin to wonder if that
isn't why your father left the house empty all these
years.'

'What a pity you can't ask him,' he drawled. 'Unless you can communicate with the dead. Can you?'

'No.'

'Then we'll never know. Do you mind?'

'Mind what? Not being able to communicate with
the dead?' she asked flippantly.

'No,' he denied patiently, 'being thought my partner.'

'No, why should I? Do you?'

'No. I'll be at the hospital if you need me.' Pushing
open the garden door, he walked out.

Eyes slightly unfocused, Claris stared after him for
a moment. No help there. Had she expected it? No,
she thought wryly. She was paid to solve his problems, big or small. She suspected this problem wasn't
going to be small. And it was all her own fault; she
should have treated Mrs Staple Smythe with the def-

erence she clearly expected. Maybe explained that Adam was paranoid about his privacy.

Partner? She gave a half-laugh. She doubted *any-one* would seriously think her his partner. Not that she wanted to be. The attraction she felt for him was entirely reluctant and very, very unwanted. A complication she didn't need. Adam wouldn't be attracted to someone like herself in a million years, and if he ever discovered how she felt... Dismissing it, suppressing it, she turned away. Funny how things turned out, though. At school all she had wanted out of life was to be a games mistress. She'd done her teacher training, but had then been unable to find a post. Several temporary jobs later, she had discovered a rather bewildering ability in herself to understand computer systems and the stock market. Figures, numbers, information technology, were as familiar to her now as her own face. A far cry from hockey sticks.

She had also discovered that she had an extraordinary talent to make money. One day she would be rich. Not as rich as Adam Turmaine, perhaps, but maybe not far behind. Tempting offers from top companies had come her way, all of which she had turned down. To work for Adam. She still didn't know if she'd been wise. She'd convinced herself she could cope with the attraction she felt for him, and so far she had managed just that. But living in the house with him, being with him constantly, was straining her feelings to the limit.

With a little sigh, she picked up the phone and rang Neville at the London office.

'You look nice,' Adam commented.

She crossed her eyes at him.

'You do,' he insisted. 'Purple is perhaps not *totally* your colour...'

'It's burgundy.'

'Oh.'

She laughed. 'I don't have many eveningy things.'

'Best get yourself some, then. Feeling better?'

She gave him a look of puzzlement.

'You were angry earlier.'

'Oh, not really angry,' she confessed. 'More cross with myself. I encountered Mrs Staple Smythe and one of her cronies in Rye this morning. She—annoyed me.' She'd more than annoyed her; she'd deliberately parked across Claris's car in the car park preventing her from leaving. She couldn't *prove* it was deliberate, though, and she hadn't known at first that it was Mrs Staple Smythe's car.

'I don't want to be bothered with it, Claris.'

She gave a small smile. 'You think I don't know that? And give that here before you break it.'

He obediently extended his wrist for her to fit his cufflink. 'What would I do without you?'

'Find some other poor fool.'

'Is that how you think of yourself?' he asked quietly. He sounded abnormally serious.

'No, and if you don't hurry up we'll be late.'

Pulling a face, he turned away to pick up his jacket and slip it on. 'Did I tell you that Arabella was coming down?' he asked casually.

'No,' she denied drily, and neither by look, nor deed did she let him see how jealousy curled unwanted in her insides. 'When?'

'Tomorrow.'

'I'll take Nathan out for the day,' she offered. 'Is she staying the night?'

Amusement in his brown eyes, he shook his head. 'Don't know. Ready?'

'As I'll ever be. Who's driving?'

'You are.' Handing her her car keys, he escorted her out. 'How are you getting on with Lydia?'

'Fine, we understand each other very well.'

'Good.'

She knew that he meant it. Lydia had worked for him a long time. First in Wiltshire, where he'd lived after leaving university, and then London. He was very fond of his housekeeper, and if you didn't get on with her, then that was your problem, not hers. Fortunately, Lydia hadn't taken her in aversion either. She hadn't taken to *Arabella*, but Claris didn't know why. She quite liked the other girl. She hadn't expected to, but she did. Empty-headed maybe, but pretty and amusing. She and Adam had been seeing each other off and on for ages. She didn't entirely understand the *attraction*, but then, it was none of her business.

Parking, as instructed, down by the Quay, she collected her bag and wrap, locked the car, and they walked slowly up Mermaid Street towards the ancient and famous inn. Walking carefully, because of the cobbles, she murmured quietly, 'I like Rye.'

'So do I.'

'I went into the Heritage Centre this morning and sat through seven hundred years of its history. They have the most amazing town model. Sound and light effects to capture the imagination. It was very well done.'

'Good.'

She smiled and passed through the heavy door he was holding for her.

Adam nodded to the desk clerk, gave his name, and they were directed to a small room at the end of a narrow corridor. Mark Davies and his wife were already there. They both looked nervous.

Two hours and a great many scribbles on the tablecloth later, Adam glanced at Claris, and she nodded.

'I'll get my lawyer to draw up details,' he told the other man.

'You'll fund it?' he asked almost in disbelief. 'Just like that?'

'Yes.' Taking his business card from his pocket, Adam scribbled a number on the back. 'Ring him tomorrow...'

'Tomorrow's Saturday...' Mark began. Adam just looked at him, and the other man gave a nervous smile.

'His name's Andrew Delane. He'll deal with everything. Don't discuss it with anyone else.'

'No.'

With a faint smile, Adam held out his hand, and Mark grasped it as though it was a lifeline. Which it probably was. All his hopes and dreams rested on that handshake.

Taking Claris by the elbow, Adam escorted her out. She turned once to smile at the young couple before she was urged outside.

Instead of turning left, Adam moved her to the right, through a heavy door, and into a small bar at the rear of the inn with a fireplace big enough to roast an ox. Looking round her with interest, she briefly examined the oak beams, crossed swords, and some rather nice carvings, but what seemed bizarre were the rather modern lamps set in the fireplace.

'What will you have? More orange juice?' he asked with a rather wicked glint in his eye.

'Seeing as I'm driving,' she agreed drily, 'yes.'

'Find yourself somewhere to sit.'

Easier said than done; the place was obviously very popular. The door to the garden stood open, and she headed in that direction. A small table became vacant just as she reached it and she hastily sat, her back to the inn wall. Putting her bag and wrap on the other chair, to keep it free, she stared at the other couples who had also chosen the fresh air.

Her mind on the young couple they had just left, she only gradually became aware of the hissed conversation going on between two young women who were sitting somewhere behind her.

'That's Adam Turmaine.'

'Who?'

'Adam Turmaine! My mother knows his aunt's cleaner. He's living with that redhead that just went outside. Unmarried mother with some sort of hold over him. Apparently,' the first woman whispered, 'she won't let anyone see him. Mrs Staple Smythe…'

'Who?'

'Oh, you won't know her,' she said dismissively. 'She's a friend of his aunt, but she was apparently absolutely furious at not getting in to see him. Said the redhead blocked all attempts. Didn't even tell him she was *there*!'

'Perhaps she's a control freak!'

Control freak? Astonished, Claris leaned even further back, in order to hear better.

'I wouldn't mind controlling him,' the woman's friend giggled. 'He is *gorgeous*!'

'Perhaps he likes domineering women.'

'Bondage!'

Claris bit her lip.

'You never can tell with people,' one of the girls said sagely. 'I mean, she wasn't even pretty.'

'Well, you know what they say. You don't look at the—'

'Linda!' her friend exclaimed, sounding scandalised, and they both dissolved into muffled laughter.

'Mum said Bernice...'

'Who?'

'Mrs Turmaine's niece,' she explained impatiently. 'Mum said she'd marked him out for herself.' There was more giggling, and then, 'Perhaps she'll try to get rid of her.'

'How?'

'God knows. Perhaps she'll get her aunt to get Mrs Staple Smythe to hire a hit man. She apparently does *everything* Harriet Turmaine tells her.'

Interesting, Claris thought.

'Why would she get Mrs Staple Smythe to do it?'

'Because old SS apparently knows everything about *everybody*. And if anyone was likely to know of a hit man, she would. Shh, he's coming.'

Claris imagined them both smiling at him. She doubted Adam would even notice. Whatever else he was, he certainly wasn't conceited. She doubted he ever considered the fact that women found him attractive. Certainly he never seemed to have considered that his assistant might find him so.

Quickly moving her things, so that he could sit down, she suddenly saw a couple move from another table and hastily got to her feet in order to grab it before someone else could. She didn't want Adam overhearing any interesting conversations.

Her employer didn't even look surprised at her sudden move, merely followed her and sat down.

'Good boy,' she praised.

He slanted her a look of pure mockery.

'Tell me,' she urged almost conspiratorially, 'have you ever considered bondage?'

CHAPTER TWO

'FREQUENTLY. Keep a close eye on them, will you?'

'Mark and Sara? Yes, of course. I shall be a veritable aunty,' she promised him.

'He doesn't know how clever he is.'

'Of course he doesn't. He thinks anyone with computer literacy could do what he does. I thought I might make a tape.'

'Tape?'

'Keep up, Adam,' she reproved lightly, 'I've changed the subject. I thought I might make a tape of Nathan's chatter for Paul and Jenny.' With a little smile, she added, 'Doesn't stop, does he? Talking away to himself. Could almost be a foreign language. I thought it might help. No one really knows how much unconscious people can hear or understand.'

'No. You're in a very frivolous mood.'

'Must be the orange juice. Is he a fighter?'

'Paul? Yes, I would say so.'

'Tell me about him.'

'Tell you what? That he's a fitness fanatic? Much good it did him.'

'It will help,' she said gently.

'Yes,' he sighed. 'I find it very hard. I talk to him, tell him about the baby, about how Jenny's parents are doing. Hospitals are such—depressing places.' Sipping his drink, he continued almost absently, 'We've been friends since university. Best man at his

41

wedding. Nathan's godfather. I don't think I can bear the thought that he might never know what Paul was like. *Is* like,' he corrected hastily, as though even to think the worst might be prophetic.

'Then it will be up to you to tell him, won't it?' she asked gently. 'It's only been just over a week, Adam. A week isn't long for someone to be in a coma.'

'No.'

With nothing further to say on the subject, because there was nothing they *could* say, and her frivolity quite gone, they both watched a young couple walk out into the garden and take the table Claris had so recently vacated. The husband—boyfriend, lover, whatever—courteously seated his lady, and Claris gave a wry smile. Catching Adam's rather sardonic eye, her smile widened. She knew exactly what he was thinking: that *she* was thinking he should have done the same. 'No,' she denied softly. 'You don't seat furniture.'

'And is that how you think of yourself? As part of the furniture?'

'It's how I think you think of me,' she corrected.

'And couldn't care less?'

'And couldn't care less,' she agreed, although she wasn't quite sure if that was true. She didn't *expect* anything of him, and so wasn't disappointed when she didn't get it. It wasn't his fault she found him attractive.

'Do you have a boyfriend?'

Forcing herself to sound amused, she said, 'I've had several.'

'That isn't what I asked.'

Giving in, she shook her head. 'Not at the moment.'

'Don't you want to marry? Have children?'

'Maybe. One day.' At the back of her mind she supposed there had always been the vague idea that one day she would marry, have little ones, but until she had begun looking after Nathan that was all it had been—vague. Nathan had rather changed that, reminded her that her biological clock was ticking.

'You can invite anyone to the house. You know that, don't you?'

'Thank you,' she said drily.

He gave a small smile. 'I don't know very much about your personal life, do I?'

'No. Why should you want to? Feeling guilty about burying me in the country?' And then she realised something she should have realised earlier. 'That was why you agreed to go to Mrs Staple Smythe's awful party, wasn't it? So that I could meet the locals. Make friends.'

'Is it?'

'Yes,' she said positively. 'It was a nice thought.'

'I don't have nice thoughts,' he denied mildly.

'Yes, you do. What a pity it turned out to be so disastrous.'

'Mmm,' he agreed wryly.

A faint smile in her eyes, she reassured him, 'I'm a big girl, Adam; you don't need to—consider me.'

'Be pretty damned selfish not to.'

'You are pretty damned selfish,' she retorted, laughing. 'But thank you for the thought. If I want to go out, I'll ask.' Changing the subject again, prompted by the overheard conversation, she said, 'I didn't notice any fluttery behaviour from your aunt. Quite the opposite, in fact. You said your memory of her was of a woman who couldn't string two sentences together.'

'Must have been someone else,' he answered, his eyes lighting with amusement.

She wondered if she ought to tell him that Harriet apparently controlled Mrs Staple Smythe, and then decided not to. He had enough on his mind with Paul and Jenny. 'Heard anything from Bernice?' she asked naughtily.

He stared at her for a moment whilst he obviously searched his memory, and then a look of enlightenment dawned. Spurious, she knew. Adam's memory was phenomenal, despite his pretence to the contrary. Details that other people often dismissed as irrelevant he stored in his very fertile mind. It was what made him so dangerous, and so attractive. 'The young woman at the party? No,' he denied. 'Should I have done?'

'Not necessarily.' Although if her unknown informants were to be believed he would soon be doing so. Searching his bland face, she teased softly, 'Don't want to know why I asked?'

'I'm sure you'll tell me if you think it important.'

'Mmm,' she agreed amiably. 'What was your uncle like?'

He pulled a face. 'I don't honestly know. He and my father didn't get on. Rather a self-important man, I think. Judgemental. Why?'

'Just curious,' she said mildly. 'What time is Arabella coming tomorrow?'

'Don't know. Want another drink?'

'No, thanks.'

'Then let's make a move.'

Which meant she had probably begun to bore him. Finishing her drink, she stared round her whilst he finished his. They were mostly young couples in the garden, some with their arms round each other, and just for a moment she felt envy. For once the summer air was warm, and as darkness fell it brought an intimacy that felt—sad. Fool, she scolded herself. She had never been a romantic, which was no doubt why she found her unwanted feelings for Adam so hard to put into perspective. Remembering the conversation she had overheard earlier, she began to smile. Control freak. Perhaps she was.

'Why the smile?'

'I was wondering if I was a control freak.'

He looked at her, gave a disbelieving shake of his head at her odd behaviour, and got to his feet.

Collecting her things, she joined him. With no need to go back through the inn, they walked out through the garden. 'Do you remember the first time we met?' she asked him as they negotiated the uneven cobbles.

'Vaguely.'

'You asked if I cried easily.'

'Did I? How extraordinary.'

'No, it isn't,' she denied. 'You made them all cry. The Sallys and the Janes...'

'But not you.'

'No, not me. I appear to be shout-proof.'

'I don't shout.'

No, he just made people feel stupid.

'Neither do I suffer fools. And some of them were very foolish indeed.'

Yes, so she'd heard. Falling in love with him, trying to attract him, crying when he reproved them over some mistake. He'd had a lot of assistants over the years, both male and female, and none of them had lasted very long. She'd worked for him for six months. Sometimes it felt like for ever, as though she had always known him, known what he was like— and she suddenly had a mental image of herself still working for him when she was an old, old lady. Unmarried, efficient, his right hand. Spinster. Unfulfilled.

'Keys?'

With a little blink, she hastily fumbled for her car keys. She hadn't even noticed that they'd reached the car. 'Sorry—wool-gathering.'

They drove home in silence. Silence inside the car, silence out. Theirs seemed to be the only car on the road. The warm breeze through the open windows was somehow soothing.

Parking by the stable block, she lingered a moment to stare up at the sky. The stars were brighter here, more important, and she stretched her arms up, savoured for a moment the utter tranquillity. A fox barked nearby and she shivered.

'Time to go in,' he said quietly. He sounded as reluctant as she felt to end the evening. She wondered why. It was just an evening like so many others. Maybe it was because it felt like summer at long last. A warm, magical evening when anything might happen. And never had she been so conscious of a man's warmth beside her.

Slowly locking the car, an unfamiliar yearning swept over her, and was hastily dismissed as she followed Adam into the house. Leaving him to lock up, she said a quiet goodnight and went upstairs to her room.

It seemed to take a long time to get to sleep, and, when she did finally manage it, it seemed no time at all before she was woken abruptly by the shrilling phone.

Only half awake, she glanced at the clock, groaned when she saw it was barely six, and without bothering to put on her robe hurried to answer it. It was the hospital.

Replacing the receiver, she went to tap on Adam's door. Receiving no answer, she cautiously opened it and peeped inside. The bed covers were turned back, the bed empty. Hearing the unmistakable sounds of his shower, she walked across and rapped sharply on the bathroom door.

She heard the shower turned off, and then the door was wrenched open with such speed that she nearly toppled inside. Wet and naked, a small towel round his hips, Adam stared at her in disbelief and—disappointment?

Not giving herself time to think about it, about him, she explained in her quiet way, 'The hospital just rang. Paul's awake.'

As though he hadn't heard, his eyes still fixed on hers, he continued to stare at her, and then he sighed and sagged against the doorframe. 'Thank God.' Briefly closing his eyes, he repeated, 'Thank God.' Water was dripping from his hair down his face and he irritably wiped it away. 'Did they say anything else?'

Forcing her mind into focus, forcibly dismissing

everything else, she shook her head. 'Not much. Just that he was awake, that he was confused and agitated, and they thought it might help if you went over.'

'I'm on my way. Thanks, Claris.'

Turning away, she went back to her own room and closed the door, leaning back against it. His reaction when he'd opened the door to her stayed in her mind. How often had it happened? she wondered. His past female assistants coming into his room uninvited? More than once she would have guessed, judging by the expression on his face when he'd seen her there. Before she'd explained, his immediate thought had been Not again, hadn't it? Although what his previous assistants had been doing in his home was anyone's guess. But if she'd ever needed confirmation that her attraction for him would never be reciprocated, then she'd got it, hadn't she? He would be horrified if he ever learned that his present assistant was far from indifferent. Not that he ever would, she vowed. Not from her, anyway.

Straightening, her face solemn, she caught a glimpse of her reflection in the long cheval mirror in the corner of her room. No robe, a skimpy nightdress that revealed more than it covered—and he'd been naked. And he would never know, she thought with wry self-mockery, how, just for an instant, she had been tempted to touch her fingers to that naked wet chest. She had never allowed herself to imagine intimacy with him. If any such thoughts ever did intrude, they were hastily squashed. She always avoided saying or doing anything that might be misconstrued. She teased him, answered back, pretended. For her own sake as well as his. But seeing him just now…

She'd been startled, that was all, she tried to tell herself. Still warm from her bed, half-asleep, and a little hormonal urge had kicked in. Perhaps she was frustrated. Perhaps she ought to find herself a man.

With a despairing sigh, a little shake of her head, she went to have her own shower. Erotic thoughts were OK, she assured herself. Erotic thoughts were entirely normal. And sometimes, she thought with a forced grin, her thoughts were very erotic indeed. But not about Adam. Adam was a no-go area. He wasn't for her. She *knew* that, and on a logical level she didn't *want* him for herself. He wasn't her sort of person at all.

Yes, he was. Don't lie to yourself, Claris, don't ever do that. She just wished she hadn't seen him naked, because now the image wouldn't go away.

She was still thinking about it when she went downstairs to make herself a coffee. With her hair tied on top of her head for coolness, and wearing loose cotton trousers and top, she threw open the kitchen window and leaned her elbows on the sill. The sky was blue, the larks were singing, and all must be well in the world of a control freak. *Must* be. *Had* to be.

'You're up early.'

Turning, she forced a smile for the housekeeper.

'Woke you as well, did he? Where's he gone at this unearthly hour?'

'The hospital. No, it's all right,' she assured hastily as she saw Lydia's face change. 'Paul woke up.'

Her shoulders slumped, and she whispered thankfully, 'Thank God.' Turning away, she began filling the percolator.

Staring at the rigid back, the grey hair pulled back

into an old-fashioned bun, Claris knew that the house-keeper's bluntness hid a very kind heart. She wasn't a communicator, and perhaps she found it hard to chatter about inconsequential things, but Claris liked her and felt comfortable with her. Claris remembered her earlier curiosity, and asked, 'Did any of my predecessors ever stay in his home?'

'Sometimes,' Lydia answered absently, 'if he was busy. Not often, mind—and certainly not after Jane.'

'Oh, dear. What did Jane do?'

'Pursued him. Funny how he didn't think twice about asking you down here.'

No, it wasn't funny at all. 'He knows I won't pursue him,' she said quietly.

'Very wise,' Lydia agreed softly and with rather an odd smile on her face. 'He likes to do his own chasing. What time's Madam coming?'

'Madam?' she asked in bewilderment as she puzzled over Lydia's smile.

'*Arabella!*'

'Oh, my goodness, I'd forgotten all about her.'

'Then perhaps you'd better ring her and tell her not to come.'

Back in control again, Claris denied comically, 'Oh, no, no, no. I never get involved in Adam's personal life. If he wants to put her off he can ring her from the hospital. Anyway, he might be back before she arrives.'

He wasn't. Claris was playing with the baby in the lounge when she arrived.

'Hello, Claris—oh, how sweet,' Arabella cooed as she hurried in, and promptly sat down beside Nathan. 'Is he yours?' Without waiting for an answer she began piling bricks up for him. 'Lydia says Adam isn't here.'

'No, he had to go out. I don't know how long he'll be.'

'I'll wait,' she said with a slightly worried air. 'I have to tell him something. What's his name?'

'Nathan.'

'Hello, Nathan. There's a clever boy,' she praised as he promptly knocked down the tower she'd just built. 'Claris?'

'Mmm?'

'I'm getting married,' she blurted.

Shocked, alarmed by the horror she felt, and then guilty, Claris stared at the other girl in disbelief. 'To *Adam*?'

'Adam? No,' she denied somewhat sadly. 'Alistair. I'm thirty-two, Claris, and all I ever wanted was to get married and have babies.'

'And Adam won't marry you?' she asked gently.

'No. But then, I always knew that. He never pretended.'

'I thought you loved him.'

'Yes, but I'm very fond of Alistair. Will he be angry, do you think?'

'Adam? I don't know. He doesn't discuss his private life with me, Arabella. Mind, he bites,' she added as Nathan began his familiar lunge.

'Oh.' Hastily sitting the baby back down, Arabella smoothed out her skirt. 'He's utterly selfish, you know...'

'Adam?' Claris enquired. It was sometimes a little confusing talking to Arabella. She never seemed to stick to one subject, just grasshoppered about. Claris gave a wry smile, because she sometimes did that herself. Most women did.

'I don't think I ever really understood why he went out with me. I'm not very clever. I sometimes don't even know what he's talking about.'

'You're very pretty,' Claris commented inadequately, because she was: blonde and blue-eyed with a willowy figure.

'Yes,' she agreed simply, 'but beauty isn't everything, is it? I sometimes think I'd rather be smart. You'd have to be smart to keep someone like Adam. He hasn't been to see me for ages…'

'He's been very busy—' Claris began.

Arabella gave a sad smile. 'You don't need to make excuses for him. I've begun to bore him; I know that. I can only talk about silly things, gossip… I have *tried* to improve my mind…'

'Oh, Arabella,' Claris exclaimed softly.

'I know. Silly, isn't it? To want someone so much that you try to change. But it didn't do any good.'

'And so you're going to marry Alistair?'

'Yes. I'm very fond of him. I expect I'll learn to love him. People do, don't they? He has the loveliest house…'

Not quite sure what to say, Claris watched Arabella as she scooted a little car about the floor for Nathan to follow. Lydia said she was foolish and empty-headed, and maybe she was, but there was no malice in her, no guile. Mrs Staple Smythe would have adored her. Brought up to be decorative, obedient, she would grace any man's home. But without love? 'Does Alistair love you?'

'Oh, yes,' she said simply, and then laughed and clapped her hands as Nathan took the car from her and pushed it himself. Nathan also clapped his hands, and she beamed at him as though he was the cleverest little boy in the whole world. 'He wasn't only seeing me, you know.'

'Wasn't he?'

'No. Women adore him.' And, to Claris's horror, Arabella's eyes filled with tears. 'I'd grow old loving him, Claris, old and never loved back. I can't bear the thought of that.'

'No.'

Looking up, she gave a wan smile.

'Does he know how you feel? Adam, I mean?'

'No. I've always pretended that I'm like him. But I'm not. I haven't lied to Alistair; you mustn't think that. I've told him about Adam…'

Oh, dear.

'And he still wants to marry me, and so I'm going to. I was going to write to Adam, but then I thought that wasn't a very nice thing to do. You have to tell someone to their face, don't you?' she asked earnestly. 'Not that he'll be upset or anything. I expect he'll just wish me well and ask what I want as a wedding present. He's very generous.'

Was he? Yes, Claris supposed he might be, and was surprised by the anger she felt. He wasn't a fool; he *must* know how Arabella felt about him. Arabella was no actress. She couldn't hide a pin under an elephant.

'I don't know what to say to you,' Claris confessed helplessly.

'Just wish me happy. You've always been very kind to me.'

'Oh, Arabella,' she exclaimed, 'you aren't hard to be kind to.'

'No, but you don't get impatient with me. Jane did. Did you know Jane? She worked for Adam before you. She was in love with him too. He got rid of her. He can be very ruthless.'

'Yes.'

'But kind. When he heard the way Jane spoke to me—all sort of superior, you know?—he was angry.' As Arabella returned her attention to the baby, Claris watched her, hoped, somehow, that she would be happy with her Alistair.

She stayed for lunch, which they ate in the garden, and when Adam still hadn't returned by the time Claris took Nathan upstairs for his nap, Arabella decided to leave him a note after all.

'Will you make sure he gets it?'

'Yes, of course.'

'Tell him I'm sorry not to tell him face to face.'

'I will.'

'Will you come to the wedding if I ask you? You could meet Alistair.'

'I'd like that. Thank you.' Almost taking herself by surprise, Claris leaned forward to kiss Arabella on the cheek. 'Drive safely.'

'Yes. How do I get out of here again?'

'Turn right at the end of the drive, second left to the end, then right onto the main road.'

'Gone, has she?' Lydia asked as Claris walked into the kitchen.

'Yes.'

'And whatever he sees in her I'll never know.'

'Don't be unkind,' Claris reproved. 'She's nice.'

'She doesn't have a brain.'

'Yes, she does—it just doesn't work like everyone else's.'

'And that's a fact! You're worth ten of her.'

Astonished by such unaccustomed praise, Claris just looked at her.

'Surprised you, have I?'

'Yes,' Claris agreed weakly.

'He should marry you.'

'*Marry* me?' she demanded in astonishment. 'Whatever for?'

'Because you'd be good for him.'

Forcing down a very odd sense of panic, she managed a smile that felt sickly. 'I doubt it. I doubt he'll ever marry.'

'He will,' Lydia said positively. 'Seen the way he baths that baby?'

'No, and what's that got to do with anything?'

'A lot. I probably know him better than anyone.'

She felt decidedly weak, on the edge of a ridiculous panic, so she sat herself at the kitchen table. Accepting the cold drink Lydia placed before her, she asked stupidly, 'How does he bath the baby?'

Lydia grinned. 'Energetically. He's like a child.'

'*Adam* is?'

'Mmm. Boats—I ask you. He makes more mess than the baby does.'

'Boats?'

'Four of them. Underwater, overwater, paddle steamer, something that spouts water. Take a look in his bathroom.'

'Certainly not.'

Lydia laughed. 'Are you *really* immune to all his charm?'

'What charm?' Claris asked dismissively as she finally managed to suppress her feelings.

'He's different with you,' Lydia added quietly.

'Different from what?'

'All the others who've worked for him. He likes you.'

'I'm a very likeable person,' she retorted flippantly, and was extraordinarily grateful when she heard Nathan begin to wake.

Unclipping the baby alarm, she hurried upstairs and into the baby's room, and concentrated solely on Nathan. Leaning on the cot rail, she stared down at his laughing face. ''Hello, pumpkin.'

'Eben.'

'I'm sure you're right. And what's all this I hear about boats?'

He shrieked, and like a piece of quicksilver he rolled over and hauled himself up on the bars. 'Dad, dad, dad. Dib.'

'Dib to you too. Come on, smiley one.'

Halfway across the landing, she suddenly halted and veered off towards Adam's room. Feeling like an interloper, she peeped into his bathroom. Four boats sat along the edge of the bath. And one yellow plastic duck. Nathan lunged, and she hastily hauled him into a safer position.

'You're not the cuddliest of babies, are you?' she asked him as she retreated. 'Like holding an eel. Want to go for a walk?'

Halting his struggles, he looked at her, and she

laughed. 'Know that word, do you?' Staring into big blue eyes, she thought she was probably in love with him. Certainly she had this ridiculous urge to keep touching him. 'What will I do when you leave?' she asked him softly. And, please God, he *would* leave. It would be a long haul though, wouldn't it, before his parents were ready to be discharged from hospital? The baby lunged for the light fitting above her head and she hastily grabbed him. 'The sooner you learn to walk, my friend, the safer we'll all be. Come on.'

Carrying him carefully downstairs, she put her head into the kitchen. 'I'm going to take Nathan out in the pram for some fresh air.'

'Can you go past the shop? I need some baking soda.'

'Yes, of course. Anything else?'

'No, I don't think so.'

With a smile, Claris retreated and carried the baby out to the stable block, where his pram was parked. She hadn't known people still *used* baking soda. 'Just goes to show what *I* know about cooking,' she told the laughing baby.

Buckling him in, she made sure his sunshade was properly fixed and wheeled him down the path and out into the lane.

His laughter put a smile on her face, and the way he waved his hands and chattered made her feel extraordinarily maternal. Forcing herself *not* to think of Lydia's words she pushed him down to the small convenience store. Not wanting to leave him outside, she awkwardly manoeuvred the pram through the narrow door. A big freezer stood to the left, and on the right was a stand holding birthday cards and another holding newspapers. All the rest of the goods were stacked behind the counter.

'Good afternoon.' Claris smiled at the man behind the wooden barrier.

He nodded to her.

'Do you have any baking soda?'

'Yes…'

'No,' a female voice denied hastily from somewhere out of sight. Almost immediately a woman emerged from behind the shelves. Face pink, she looked awkward and embarrassed. 'No,' she repeated. Ignoring the man's obvious astonishment, she continued hurriedly, 'All our stock is ordered for our customers.'

Slightly nonplussed, Claris murmured inadequately, 'Oh. You don't sell anything that isn't ordered?'

'No.'

Looking from one to the other, she asked, 'But you could order something for me if I asked?'

'It would be quicker to drive into Rye.'

Disbelieving, beginning to get an inkling of what was going on, she asked pleasantly, 'So any passing stranger would be unable to purchase anything?'

'Yes.'

'A funny way to run a shop. It isn't, by any chance, owned by a Mrs Staple Smythe, is it?' she asked softly. The woman went red; the man just looked bewildered. 'OK,' Claris agreed. 'Sorry to have troubled you.'

The man opened his mouth as if to say something; the woman glared him into silence. Neither offered to hold the door for her as she awkwardly got herself out.

Walking further along the lane, so that she could do a complete circuit of the village, her face thoughtful, Claris stared at the impressive houses. There was a great deal of money here, which, in turn, brought a great many privileges. What it didn't do, of course, was turn a mean spirit into a better one. If, indeed, Mrs Staple Smythe *was* behind this. She could only assume that being refused service in the shop was a punishment of some kind. Because Mrs Staple Smythe hadn't been able to get to see Adam? 'She doesn't know how lucky she was,' she told a delighted-looking Nathan. 'Your godfather would have decimated her.' Or was it because they thought her an unmarried mother? Because her face didn't fit? What else would they try?

Ignoring her, she discovered. Everyone she passed deliberately, and very obviously, turned their backs. Not that there were *many*, it was a small village after all, but all four women she passed ignored her. How very pathetic and childish. It was also foolish. Petty victimisation wouldn't make her leave; it would just make her more determined to stay.

Pushing the pram along the lane, she refused to look back. She gave a soft laugh as she surprised a man in his garden. He'd obviously forgotten his instructions, because instead of turning his back he just stared at her.

'Good day,' she greeted him pleasantly.

Presumably horrified at such a social solecism, he rushed to his side gate and slammed it behind him.

Laughing delightedly, she walked on. Maybe it was

all unconnected, she surmised. Maybe the people in the village behaved this way to *all* strangers. If she hadn't overheard that conversation in the inn how would she have interpreted it? That they were all daft, probably, and she would have laughed. 'So, we'll laugh,' she told the baby. 'Won't we?'

Nathan obediently laughed. 'Quite right,' she told him, 'and my conversational abilities are going to go severely downhill if I spend all my time talking to you.'

Turning the corner, she began walking back towards Grays Manor. She had heard of strangers never being accepted in communities, but had never encountered it first-hand. She supposed she had always assumed that if you were nice to people they would be nice back. But Harriet Turmaine hadn't been nice—although she *had* warned her, hadn't she? And Mrs Staple Smythe definitely wasn't nice. And so Claris hadn't been nice to her.

Her own fault? Possibly. She would be nice to the next person she met, she promised herself. Except that she didn't meet anybody else. The rest of the village seemed empty. Deserted. Not even a dog. Perhaps dogs weren't allowed. Perhaps *children* weren't allowed. 'We've entered the Twilight Zone,' she murmured deeply, and Nathan shrieked. Smiling at him, the sudden explosion of pain in her cheek made her gasp.

CHAPTER THREE

SHOCKED, bewildered by a pain so vicious it made her feel sick, she put a hand up to her face. It came away sticky with blood. For a moment, one startling moment, she thought she'd been shot. And then she saw the small stone lying in the pram.

Slowly picking it up, she stared at it. A child with a catapult? If it had hit the baby...

Galvanised into motion, she hurried on, staring around her as she did so. There was nothing to be seen. Nothing to be heard. No running footsteps. No whispers. Nothing. She could have been blinded. The *baby* could have been blinded. An accident, she told herself. Surely an accident. Gingerly touching her cheekbone again, she winced. A bruise was beginning to form. It hurt like hell. And if the child or whoever was still around... Almost running, she went back to the house.

The side door stood open, as it usually did when it was warm, to let the air circulate, and she wheeled the pram inside.

'Don't bring that in here—' Lydia began, and then stopped. 'What happened to your face?' she demanded.

'I don't know. A child with a catapult, I think.'

'Show me.'

'It's all right...'

'No, it isn't.' Wrenching Claris's chin up, none too

61

gently, Lydia stared at the open wound on her cheek-bone. 'It needs a stitch...'

'No, it doesn't,' Claris denied impatiently. Still shaken, she felt irritable.

'Claris. It needs a stitch.'

'What needs a stitch?' Adam asked mildly from behind them. 'And why is that pram in here?'

Without turning, irrationally angry, Claris bent to unstrap the baby. Lifting him out, she handed him to Lydia. Grabbing the pram handle, she attempted to turn it. Adam caught her arm, halted her.

He stared at her injury, his eyes deep and dark, unfathomable. 'What happened to your face?' he asked very, very softly.

'Nothing,' she denied shortly. 'And will you please let go?'

His whole demeanour might have appeared laid back, but the force with which he removed her hands from the pram before propelling her into the light from the door so that he could examine her cheek was pure steel. 'What happened?'

'Someone catapulted a stone at her,' Lydia informed him. 'It needs stitching.'

'It does not need stitching!' Claris denied crossly for what felt like the fourteenth time.

'Who?' he asked.

'I don't *know* who! Mrs Staple Smythe's hit man, probably.'

'I beg your pardon?'

'Nothing,' she said irritably. 'I was being facetious.'

The baby suddenly burst into tears, and they all

looked at him in guilty astonishment. Nathan never cried.

'Oh, darling, it's all right,' Lydia soothed. 'Hush, hush. Come on, you come with Nanna. We'll go and get you a nice drink.'

'Nanna?' Adam enquired, at his most urbane.

'Yes,' she agreed defiantly. 'Nanna.' Carrying the baby towards the kitchen, she ordered over her shoulder, 'And take her to the hospital.'

'I don't want to go to the hospital,' Claris muttered.

'And did I ever take notice of what you wanted?' Adam enquired. 'It could have taken your eye out.'

'Or the baby's,' she whispered, and only then did it truly come home to her what might have happened. It wasn't the injury to herself that upset her so, but the thought that it might have been Nathan. All the colour draining from her face, she put out a hand to clutch at Adam's shirt-front.

He grabbed a small antique chair from one side and shoved it beneath her. 'Sit,' he ordered.

'I'm all right...'

'You are *not* all right.' Forcing her down, he instructed, 'Put your head between your knees.'

'I'm not going to *faint*!' she argued crossly.

'But it is all right to,' he said softly. 'You don't have to be tough *all* the time.'

Astonished, she just stared at him, and then took a deep, shaky breath as he crouched in front of her.

'A little human frailty is allowed,' he mocked gently.

'Yes,' she agreed, suddenly unable to look at him. 'It was the thought of Nathan being injured. When

it's someone else's child, when you're responsible...
I'm all right now.'

'Sure?'

She nodded.

'Then go and wait in the car.' Standing, he helped
her to her feet, and as she turned to go out she nearly
walked into an elderly, tall, thin gentleman just coming in.

'Sorry,' she muttered automatically as she stepped
back.

'Saw what happened,' he said gruffly. 'Vandalism.
Strike whilst the iron's hot and all that. Looks nasty.
Best get it seen to.' Shoving out his hand, nearly
knocking Claris backwards, he introduced himself
brusquely. 'Colonel Davenport. Courtesy title, of
course, been out of the army for years.' Looking past
Claris, he demanded, 'You Turmaine?'

'Yes,' Adam agreed. 'You saw who did it?'

'No. Can't run like I used to,' he excused, in the
same brusque voice. 'Saw where it came from,
though. Got my letter, did you?'

'Yes, but I have no time to discuss it now,' Adam
said, with a firmness that most people, if they were
wise, took notice of. 'I need to take Miss Newman to
the hospital.'

The Colonel nodded, as though in approval. 'Quite
right. First things first. Don't worry about ringing the
law; I'll do it.' Turning on his heel, his stick tap-
tapping against his leg, he walked out.

'Someone spoke to me,' Claris said in a tone of
great marvel. 'Amazing.'

'Vindicated,' Edward murmured as if he hadn't
heard her.

She glanced round at him. 'Sorry?'

'Vindicated,' he repeated. He sounded amused. 'You're being slow, Miss Newman. Not like you. He wrote to me about vandalism, didn't he?'

'Oh, yes.'

'And now he has evidence. You. Poor, poor Miss Newman.'

'Oh, shut up,' she said disagreeably. 'And I can drive myself to the hospital.'

'*I* will drive you to the hospital. I'll be two minutes.'

With a long sigh, still feeling a bit shaky, she walked out to where Adam's car was parked. It wasn't locked, and so she climbed into the passenger seat. Tilting the rearview mirror towards her, she stared at her cheek, and grimaced. The cut was bigger than she'd expected. No wonder it hurt. Taking a tissue from her pocket, she dabbed ineffectually at the blood, wincing as she did so.

'Not very hygienic,' Adam remarked as he climbed in beside her.

'It's a clean tissue,' she defended, and then sighed again. 'You don't need to do this,' she added. 'I can easily drive myself. You've only just got *back* from the hospital.'

'Be quiet,' he said mildly. Returning the mirror to its former position, he switched on the engine and drove out.

'How was Paul?' she asked quietly.

'Confused.'

Turning to look at him, she examined his face. He looked angry. Because he was worried about his friend? 'What did the doctor say?'

'The same as he always says, that it's early days.'

'But if he's come out of the coma…'

'Yes, but they still can't rule out the possibility of brain damage. He's having another scan this afternoon.'

'Did he know you?'

'I'm not sure,' he said heavily. 'Jenny was a bit better. I told her you were making a tape.'

She nodded. 'Arabella came…'

He swore. 'I forgot all about her.'

'She left you a note.'

He glanced at her, and then swiftly back to the road.

'Where are we going?'

'Private clinic. I rang to tell them we were coming. I registered us all when I knew we were moving to Rye. I thought that if the baby needed medical care I didn't want to be waiting around in an Accident and Emergency Department.'

'Of course not.'

'Because I strongly believe that if you can afford private medicine,' he continued determinedly, 'you should pay for it and not add to the woes of the National Health Service.'

'Sorry.'

'So you should be. I'll put your behaviour down to shock. The clinic isn't far, just outside the town.'

Back to his normal acerbic self, and yet, for a moment, in the hall, he had been incredibly kind. Concerned.

Moments later he pulled into the forecourt of a small white building. A nurse was waiting to greet them. She gave Adam an interested glance, then turned her attention to Claris. With a warm, professional smile, she escorted her inside.

'I'll wait out here,' he told Claris.

Following the nurse, she was quickly assessed and then taken in to see the doctor. He was young, amiable-looking, and seemed glad of an opportunity to practise his skills.

He gave her a warm smile and seated her in the light by the window. 'Chris Markham,' he introduced himself. 'Painful?'

'Yes.'

'What was it? A stone? Mr Turmaine said something about a catapult.'

'I'm only assuming. I didn't see anyone. But it hit with such force that I doubt it was thrown. And Colonel Davenport—' Breaking off, she gave a dismissive little shake of her head. She didn't suppose the doctor would be remotely interested in the Colonel.

'I don't think the bone is chipped, but we'll X-Ray it to make sure. Are you up to date with your tetanus shots?'

'Yes,' she said promptly, and he laughed.

'When?'

She gave him a look of disgust. 'I don't really need one, do I?'

'Yes. I won't stitch it; butterfly tapes will leave less of a scar. You're going to have a black eye, I'm afraid.'

'Thank you,' she said drily.

'Doing anything tonight?' he asked casually.

Slightly nonplussed, her mind not really on what he was asking, she echoed, 'Doing anything?'

'Mmm. Would you like to come for a drink with me?'

'Oh.'

He laughed. 'Why so surprised? Don't men usually ask you out?'

'No,' she denied honestly, and then she smiled. 'I'd like that, but can we do it another night?'

'Sure,' he agreed easily. 'Give me a ring.'

'OK.'

Half an hour later she was finished, and they shook hands. 'Thank you, Dr Markham.'

'Chris,' he corrected with a smile.

'Chris,' she agreed.

The nurse escorted her back to the car park. Adam was leaning against his car, looking bored.

'Sorry I was so long,' she apologised.

'You weren't long at all. Everything all right?'

'Yes.'

Opening her door for her, which occasioned her giving him an old-fashioned look, he merely smiled again and climbed into his own side. 'You look as though you're going to have a black eye.'

'That should please SS,' she retorted without thinking.

About to turn on the ignition, he halted and turned to face her.

'Sorry,' she apologised quickly. 'I'm not feeling myself.'

'SS?'

'Nothing. No one. It's not important.' Folding her hands in her lap, eyes lowered, cursing her stupid tongue, she added quietly, 'I was being bitchy.'

'About?'

'Mrs Staple Smythe.' Glancing at him, her grey eyes serious, she explained, 'She made it very plain that she didn't like me, and so I...'

'Was just being bitchy,' he agreed.

'Yes.'

'And there's nothing else you wish to tell me?'

Like what? she wondered. That she was being ostracised? 'No,' she denied. Adam had enough on his plate without her adding to it.

He nodded and switched on the engine.

He obviously *had* heard her comment about someone speaking to her, though. It was never wise to assume Adam wasn't listening. Rolling her head on the seat-back, she stared out at the passing scenery and wondered rather idly what the doctor had seen in her that had made him want to invite her out. It wasn't her looks; she didn't have any—or none to speak of. Her charm? Her lively humour? Perhaps he just like girls with ginger hair.

'Something is amusing you?' Adam asked smoothly.

Turning her head, she gave a wan smile. 'Just thoughts. I wonder if the Colonel reported it yet?'

'I imagine he did so immediately,' he said drily. 'Not that they will be able to do very much, but if they could impress on parents the dangers of firing catapults... Don't take Nathan into the village again—nor go yourself.'

'That's absurd!' she exclaimed. 'I mean, of course I won't take the baby, but as for me...'

'I mean it, Claris.'

'But why? It was an accident—*must* have been an accident...'

'Then until we find out who's responsible, you will do as I ask. Won't you?' he added softly.

About to argue, she gave a deep sigh instead. He was the boss and it was a wise assistant who knew when to rebel—and when to give in. 'Yes,' she agreed.

'Good.'

He activated the remote control for the gates, drove inside, reactivated it, and they closed behind him. Parking by the stable block, he switched off the engine.

'Get Lydia to make you a cup of tea,' he instructed as he climbed out, waited for her, then followed her into the house. 'You don't like me much, do you, Claris?' he asked quietly.

Astonished, she turned to look at him. 'Of course I like you. What on earth brought that on?'

'Old age, I expect,' he said dismissively. 'Go on, go and get your tea.'

Puzzled, she began to walk on, then halted. 'Oh, I left Arabella's letter on the mantelpiece in the lounge for you,' she said quietly.

'Thank you.'

Without waiting to see if he went to retrieve it, she continued on to the kitchen. Nathan was in his high chair having his tea, and when he saw her he laughed and waved his arms at her.

Finding a smile, she sat at the table and watched Lydia feed him. The housekeeper gave her a searching glance, and then carried on with what she was doing. 'I'll make you a cup of tea in a minute.'

'I can do it.' But she didn't move.

'The police came.' Lydia snorted. 'Much good that will do anybody.'

'No.'

Giving Nathan the last spoonful, she handed him his bottle and went to put the kettle on.

'I didn't get your baking soda,' Claris confessed. 'Sorry.'

'It's not important. I've got to go into Rye on Monday; I'll get it then. Why don't you take your tea upstairs and have a lie-down?'

'I'm all right; it's only a cut face.'

'And shock.'

'Guilt,' she corrected honestly. 'It could so easily have hit the baby…'

'Well, it didn't, so stop blaming yourself for something that never happened.' Pouring the tea, Lydia handed Claris her cup and instructed again, 'Go and lie down. I'll call you when dinner's ready.'

Feeling it was easier to obey, Claris got to her feet. With another small smile for Nathan, she lightly kissed his hair and went up to her room. In all honesty it was a relief to be on her own. She didn't feel like talking. Putting her tea on the bedside table, she went to examine her face in the mirror. It was already going blue and puffy. And if the young doctor could ask her out looking like this, she thought, trying for some humour, she must be better than she'd thought. So why did she suddenly feel depressed? She didn't know. She really didn't think she knew.

Taking Lydia's advice, she propped herself up on the bed to drink her tea and puzzle over Adam's behaviour. Why on earth had he assumed she didn't like him? And even if he'd thought it, why ask? She wouldn't have said that he cared one way or the other. But then, she wouldn't have thought he'd like playing with boats, either.

Just sitting there thinking about it, about him, with no intention of sleeping, it came as something of a surprise when Lydia knocked on her door some two hours later and she woke with a start. And with a crick in her neck. And one eye swollen shut.

Calling out that she was awake, she swung her legs to the floor and scrambled to look in the mirror. 'Oh, nice one,' she exclaimed softly as she stared at her swollen face. Lop-sided wasn't in it. The butterfly tapes were strained tight against the swelling, and her eye was barely visible through the mounds of puffy flesh. The whole thing was a rather nice shade of blue. She'd probably frighten the baby to death.

Untying her hair from its topknot and shaking it free, she walked into the bathroom to freshen up.

Ten minutes later she walked downstairs. There was no sign of Adam, so she wandered along to the kitchen.

Lydia turned at her entrance, stared at her face, and tried to hide her smile. 'Sorry,' she apologised.

'No need,' Claris denied resignedly. 'Laughter is entirely understandable. What's for dinner? I'm starving.'

'Lamb. It's just the two of us.'

'Where did Adam go?'

'I've no idea. He bathed the baby and put him to bed, then went out.'

Perhaps he'd gone to see Arabella.

'Do you want to eat in here with me?'

'Please. Lydia?' she asked as she began to get out

knives and forks, 'Have you been in the village shop yet?'

'No, why?'

'Because the reason I didn't get your soda is because, apparently, they only keep stock that is ordered.'

Lydia glanced at her. 'Rubbish,' she said dismissively. 'No one would be daft enough to run a shop on those lines.'

'No.'

'So? What aren't you telling me?'

'I don't know, not really— except that apparently I'm not wanted here.'

'Because?'

With a soft laugh, Claris explained. 'Because I'm an unmarried mother; because—'

'They think the baby's *yours*?' Lydia exclaimed.

'Mmm.'

Lydia laughed. 'How people do love to make assumptions.'

'Yes. But I shouldn't have alienated the leading light in Wentsham society.'

Giving the younger woman a thoughtful look, the housekeeper stated, 'Which means you don't think the stone-throwing was an accident.'

'I don't know that either.' Explaining quickly about the overheard conversation in the inn, she added, 'Don't tell Adam, will you? He doesn't need anything else on his mind at the moment.'

'Not if you don't want me to. Is it bothering you?'

'No-o, not if it remains at just spitefulness, but I have the baby to consider. I don't really know what to do about it, you see. The stone and the shop could

be just isolated incidents…the stone could be anyway.
But I just thought someone else ought to know, in
case…'

'Anything else happens to you?'

She gave another soft laugh. 'Sounds awfully melo-
dramatic, doesn't it? And I don't suppose anything
will happen. I just wanted to talk about it, I think.'

'I'll keep my ears open,' Lydia promised. 'And I'll
go to the shop.'

'Thanks.'

She helped Lydia clear up the kitchen when they'd
finished eating, more for the company than any reasons of Lydia expecting help, and when the housekeeper had gone to her own room, Claris went to the
lounge. Arabella's letter had gone from the mantelpiece.

Turning on the television, she made herself comfortable in one of the squashy armchairs. After chan-
nel-hopping for a few moments, she finally settled on
the performance channel. An orchestra was playing
classical music. She had no idea what it was, but it
was pleasant and non-intrusive, and allowed her to
think. Despite her words to Lydia, she *was* bothered
about the stone-throwing. Being ignored was one
thing; being injured was entirely another. Perhaps she
ought to go and see the Colonel, talk to him about
vandalism.

And then there was Adam, who seemed to think
she didn't like him. What on earth could she have
done to give him that impression? And poor Arabella.
Perhaps Adam had gone to see her. Perhaps they were
making love… The lurch her tummy gave both
alarmed and distressed her. She shouldn't care what

Adam did, didn't *want* to care. She wished Lydia hadn't said all those things about him liking her, about how he should marry her. She didn't want to marry Adam—and Adam certainly didn't want to marry her. She could just imagine the look on his face if anyone so much as even *hinted* at it. Wishful thinking on Lydia's part... But it was getting worse, wasn't it? This continually thinking about him. She wished she'd never seen him naked.

Trying to dismiss it, she stared at the screen as the room darkened about her and tried to force her mind into other channels. And couldn't.

She didn't know what time it was when she heard the front door softly open and close; not very late, she didn't think, but she could no more stop her heart accelerating than she could stop time. All this denial and pretence was so exhausting.

'I'm in here,' she called quietly, and then wondered why she had done so. She didn't imagine Adam could care less where she was, or what she was doing. Certainly she had never called out to him before.

She heard his footsteps along the hall, and then he was standing in the doorway.

'Hi,' she said inadequately.

'Hi,' he responded neutrally. 'Waiting up for me, Claris?'

'No,' she denied.

'How are you feeling?'

'Not too bad. Arabella asked me to tell you that she was sorry not to tell you to your face.'

She just caught the white of his teeth as he smiled. 'Ah,' he agreed as he moved into the room. 'You think I've been out consoling myself?'

'I don't think I thought about it at all.' Which was a lie. She'd been thinking of nothing else whilst watching the television.

'How very wounding,' he drawled. 'Want a drink?'

'That would be nice. Gin and tonic if you have it.'

He nodded, and walked across to the drinks tray that Lydia always kept well stocked.

'Ice?'

'Please.'

He didn't bother putting on the light, for which she was grateful. There was just enough illumination from the television set and the window for him to see what he was doing. And for her to see him.

Bringing her drink across, he handed it to her, and then returned for his own. Seating himself on the long sofa to her left, he stretched out his legs and stared at the screen.

Claris continued to watch him, continued to think about Arabella's words. He *was* good-looking, and she could understand why so many women liked him. Long and lithe, indolent—and he was aware that she was watching him.

'Sibelius,' he commented softly.

'Is it?' she asked drily.

He laughed. '*Tapiola.* Violin concerto. Why are you watching it if you don't know what it is?'

'Because I like the sound. One doesn't have to be *knowledgeable* in order to like it,' she reproved him.

'True. Not going to ask where I've been?'

'No,' she denied, 'it's none of my business. Arabella invited me to her wedding,' she added casually. 'Would you mind if I went?'

'No. I might even come with you.'

'No,' she denied softly.

'No?'

'No.'

He was silent for a few moments, and then he agreed, 'Perhaps you're right.'

'I know I am.'

'And you think me totally insensitive, don't you?'

Staring down into her drink, she shook her head. 'I prefer to think that you didn't realise…'

'That she was in love with me? I assume that's what you're suggesting?'

'Yes.'

'Then, no. I didn't. You *prefer* to think that I didn't realise?'

'A slip of the tongue,' she said glibly.

'What did *she* say?' Adam asked.

'That you would wish her well and ask what she wanted as a wedding present.'

'And is that what *you* will ask *me*?' he queried almost intimately, his eyes still on the screen.

Heart accelerating again, she stared at him in shock. 'Sorry?'

'I merely wondered if that's what you would ask me. It's not important.'

Yes, it was. He seemed to be implying… 'You're getting *married*?' she whispered.

'No,' he denied easily. 'Not at the moment.'

'But you think you might?' she persisted. 'Some time in the future? But I always thought… You always said…'

'I changed my mind.' Getting up, he walked to the tray to freshen his drink. 'You sound quite shocked, Claris.'

'Yes,' she agreed dazedly 'No. I mean…oh, I don't know,' she exclaimed, disgusted with herself for her behaviour. 'It was a surprise, that was all.' Trying to pull herself together, she asked, 'Have you seen Arabella? Is that what this is about?'

'No, I had one or two things to deal with, and then I went to the hospital.'

'But you don't want Arabella to marry Alistair?' she guessed.

'On the contrary, I shall be entirely delighted if she marries him. I introduced them.'

Staring at him, she felt a little surge of anger. 'You wanted to be rid of her,' she stated.

'Yes, Claris, I wanted to be rid of her. Don't you want to know how Paul is?'

A slight edge to her voice, she asked obediently, 'How is Paul?'

'The scan was negative. They were both asleep. I just sat there for a while. Thinking.'

Planning? she wondered. She knew he could be ruthless; she had always known that. With her head resting back on the cushion, she continued to watch him. He was still standing by the drinks tray, his back to her, his newly freshened drink untouched in his hand.

'I shall miss him when he leaves,' he murmured softly.

So Arabella was history. 'Nathan?' she asked, her tone still indicative of her anger.

'Yes. The grandparents are on the road to recovery. Another few weeks and they'll be discharged.'

'And then they'll take the baby?'

'Probably. Will *you* miss him, Claris?'

'Yes. I think I went and fell in love with him.' I don't want you to be like this, she thought. Cold and uncaring. Forcing herself to neutrality, she added, 'He's a dear little chap.' Soft and sweet and happy. Ridiculously, she felt a lump form in her throat.

'Perhaps they'll let you visit him when everything is back to normal,' he said with apparent uninterest. 'Did you manage to draft out my report for Thursday's board meeting?'

'Yes, I left it on your desk.'

'Thank you.' Finally turning, he reproved quietly, 'The Arabellas of this world need someone to lean on. To have cut her adrift without support would have been needlessly cruel. And, despite your opinion to the contrary, I am not a cruel man. I like Arabella. She amuses me. And I don't pay you to judge me,' he tacked on softly.

'No. Well,' she said briskly, 'now you've put me firmly in my place, I think it's time I went to bed.' Quickly finishing her drink, she got to her feet. Walking across to him, she placed her empty glass on the tray. He caught her wrist, just gently, fingers encircling the narrow bones, and she looked at him in surprise.

He was staring at her swollen face. 'Oh, my,' he said softly. 'Oh, my, oh, my, oh, my.' His lips twitched and he moved her round so that he could see her more clearly by the light from the television. 'Black eye, did I say?' He smiled then, a warm, almost delighted smile. 'Poor baby.' And to her absolute and utter astonishment, he bent his head and kissed her full on the mouth.

CHAPTER FOUR

A SOFT, intimate, lingering kiss.

Feeling decidedly strange, and definitely off balance, Claris just looked at him, and then quickly lowered her eyes.

'I've surprised you,' he stated softly.

'Well, yes,' she agreed weakly.

'Good. Go to bed.'

'Good?' she queried. 'Why is it good to surprise me?'

'Because I so very rarely do. Go to bed,' he repeated in the same soft voice.

Yes, she thought dazedly, that seemed wise. With a last uncertain look at him, she gently tugged her wrist from his hand and walked out. Was he playing with her? A little game of reproof because she'd criticised his behaviour towards Arabella? She had no idea. For the first time since she had met him she didn't know what to think. She had always known what to think about him. Always.

'He should marry you,' Lydia had said. Halfway over the baby-gate, Claris halted. Good God, Lydia hadn't told *him* that, had she? No, of course not, she dismissed hastily as she continued on up the stairs. The woman had more sense. Hadn't she? And why think of that now? Because he'd kissed her?

You're overreacting, Claris, she told herself. Yes, of course she was. He'd seen her eye, been amused, and then he'd called her a poor baby and kissed her. It meant nothing. Absolutely nothing at all. So why couldn't she dismiss it as absolutely nothing at all? Because she was stupid, that was why. And because it had been a long time since anyone had kissed her. It hadn't even been a proper kiss. Just a gentle—lingering—touching of his mouth to hers. So why is your heart racing, Claris? Why are you out of breath? Because she'd just climbed the *stairs*, that was why.

He wasn't attracted to her; she *knew* that. If he had been he'd have been a great deal more concerned about her eye. Not call her a poor *baby*. In fact, there was *nothing* about her that attracted him. Except perhaps her mind. And she had no idea why she was attracted to him. He was rude, indifferent, manipulative, exciting—and he was thinking of getting married. To whom? Someone new? A nurse at the hospital? A doctor?

Oh, for God's sake, Claris, will you shut up about it? Quietly closing her bedroom door, she got ready for bed. And if you're so frustrated that a gentle kiss can make you behave like a loon, go find yourself a boyfriend. Ring Chris Markham at the clinic. Yes, perhaps she should.

Lying in bed, staring at the ceiling, she tried to picture the doctor's face—and saw only Adam. Naked. Finding her fingers creeping to her mouth, she snatched them away. Anyone would think she'd never been kissed before. Impatient with herself, she tried to think of something else. Her finances, work, Mrs Staple Smythe... No, not Mrs Staple Smythe. Determinedly closing her eyes—eye—she tried counting sheep. It must have worked, because when she woke up it was morning. And her eye was now completely closed.

Reluctant to face the day—face Adam—which was ridiculous, she scrambled from the bed and went to have her shower, being careful not to get the butterfly tapes wet. She rubbed her hair dry and dressed in long shorts and a loose top. It looked as though it was going to be another hot day. Slipping her feet into comfy sandals, she went down to the kitchen. Far from frightening the baby, who was sitting in his high chair, her appearance seemed to intrigue him. He stared at her, his eyes wide, and then thumped his bottle on the tray in apparent delight.

'Looks nasty,' Lydia commented. 'Sore?'

Turning to smile at her, Claris shook her head. 'No, just uncomfortable. I thought I might go and see the Colonel, ask him about vandalism.'

'Adam's already been.'

'*Adam* has?' she asked in disbelief. 'When?'

'Last night, before he went to the hospital. Do you really think he wouldn't be concerned when one of his employees is injured?'

'He didn't *behave* concerned.'

'No, because that's not his way. Egg and bacon?'

'Please.' Her mind still on Adam and his odd behaviour, she asked in bewilderment, 'But why didn't he say? He never mentioned it last night.'

'And you should know by now that Adam never tells anyone anything if he can help it.'

Alerted by the terseness in Lydia's voice, Claris stared at her. 'Are you all right, Lydia? You sound cross.'

'I'm fine,' she said shortly. 'They served Adam.'

'Pardon?' Sitting beside the baby, Claris smiled at him. But then, it was very hard not to smile at Nathan.

'The shop,' Lydia explained, almost impatiently. 'They served Adam. He went down to get the newspapers.'

'Oh, yes. Well, they would, wouldn't they? Adam's important. They have plans for him. And even though he's probably the father of my baby...'

Lydia gave a snort of laughter. 'Is he, now?'

'Mmm. Are you sure you're all right?' she asked worriedly.

'Bit of a headache,' Lydia confessed. 'I'll take some aspirins in a minute. What plans do they have for him?' she asked interestedly as she dished up Claris's breakfast.

'Lord of the Manor. Committee-sitter. And then, of course, there's Bernice. According to my unknown source in the inn, that is.'

'Bernice being...?'

'Aunt Harriet's niece.'

'Such intrigue. And I thought the country was going to be boring.'

'So did I. Has Adam eaten?'

'Yes, he's in the lounge reading the papers.' Scooping up the baby, she added, 'I'll go and get him dressed.'

'I can do it...' Claris began, but Lydia had already gone. Staring after her, a small frown in her eyes, she finally turned her attention to her breakfast, and when she'd finished sat slowly nursing a cup of tea. Lydia was no longer young. She wasn't sure *exactly* how old she was. Late sixties? And caring for a baby was hard work. Perhaps it was too much for her. Although how anyone would tell her *that* Claris didn't know. She'd mention it to Adam. Perhaps they could both do more to help.

'Is there any more of that?' he asked from behind her.

Swinging round with a little start, she stared at her employer.

He stared back, took in the magnificence of her eye, and smiled. 'Coming along nicely,' he commented. 'Tea?'

She pointed at the teapot. 'It's Sunday,' she informed him. 'My day off.'

'In other words, I pour my own tea?'

'Got it in one.' Continuing to watch him as he walked across to get a cup from the cupboard, and then pour his tea, she found that she wanted to ask him why he had kissed her. She wasn't going to, because she didn't think she would like the answer, but she would have liked to know. Dressed in jeans and a short-sleeved top, he looked fresh and clean, vitally attractive. But not for you, Claris, she told herself. No, not for her.

'What was all that about intrigue?'

'Have your ear trumpet out, did you? You must have remarkably good hearing if you could hear what we said from the lounge.'

'I have excellent hearing, and you weren't exactly whispering. So, what was it about?'

'Mind your own business,' she returned. 'You shouldn't eavesdrop on other people's conversations.' And then she laughed, because if *she* hadn't eavesdropped she wouldn't have known half of what she now knew.

Much to her surprise, he pulled out a chair and sat opposite her. 'Do you have any plans for the day?'

She shook her head. 'You?'

'I thought we might take Nathan on a picnic,' he said casually. 'Give Lydia a break.'

'Yes,' she agreed slowly, 'I was going to talk to you about that. Do you think the baby's too much for her?'

He gave her a dry glance. 'You think she would admit it if he was? Tell me why you think he might be?'

'Well, nothing concrete, only that she has a headache this morning. Picnic?' she finally registered.

'Mmm. Not a good idea?'

'I don't know.' A day with him on her own? But all her days were spent alone with him. More or less. So why was she prevaricating? Yesterday, or even the day before, she would have said immediately, Yes, sure, why not? Or made some quip about him needing help with the baby. Today, she felt—disturbed. Because things were different between them? But they weren't. Or only in her mind. Giving herself a mental shake, she nodded. 'OK, if you don't mind being seen with someone who looks as though they've been in a scrap.'

'Wear dark glasses. I'm sure the fresh air will do us the world of good,' he added laconically.

She wasn't. 'Have you been on picnics before?' she asked interestedly. 'Only it isn't something I would have imagined you doing.'

'It will be a new experience,' he told her blandly.

'Mmm. I went on one once,' she informed him, her one good eye fixed on his face. 'I completely ruined a good pair of shoes. Cow pats seemed to feature largely. And nettles.'

'Then I promise to examine the field minutely before I allow you into it. Think positively, Miss Newman. Think...'

'Adventure?' Hearing Lydia approaching, she turned to smile at her. 'We seem to be going on a picnic.'

'Oh, goody,' Lydia retorted as she handed the baby to Adam, who had to hastily push his tea out of the baby's reach. 'So long as you don't expect me to accompany you.'

'No,' Adam denied. 'You can have the day off.'

'How kind. What do you want in this said picnic?'

'I'll leave it entirely to you and Claris. Nathan and I will be in the garden.'

'Ah, women's work,' Lydia agreed sagely. 'But perhaps I should warn you that we have no lobster or champagne.'

He looked at her, a very dry expression on his face. She laughed.

Getting to his feet, he hefted the baby into a more secure position, and strolled out through the back door. Both women watched him go.

'He's never been on a picnic in his life,' Lydia commented.

'Perhaps he has a touch of sun,' Claris murmured, still rather disturbed at the thought of spending the day with him.

'A touch of something,' Lydia agreed softly, a rather thoughtful look on her face. Glancing at Claris, a glance the younger woman didn't see, Lydia gave a small smile. 'I'm sorry I was short with you earlier,' she apologised.

'It's all right.'

'No, it isn't. I don't like getting old,' she confessed. 'Well, no, that's not strictly true. It's not the old age I mind, it's all the aches and pains that accompany it...' Breaking off, she frowned as she caught movement from the hallway. 'Can I help you?' she asked coolly.

Automatically turning, Claris watched as a young woman advanced along the hall. The young woman who had been talking to Adam at the party. Bernice. Perhaps Adam was thinking of marrying *her*.

'The front door was open,' she began pleasantly.

'That doesn't give you the right to walk through it,' Lydia retorted.

'No, of course it doesn't. I did knock, but...'

'Oh, for goodness' sake, either come in or go out, girl. We don't bite.'

'No, of course you don't. You must be Lydia,' she smiled.

'Must I?'

Bernice laughed. Turning to Claris, she smiled at her. 'I was looking for Adam.'

'He's in the garden with the baby. Through that door,' she added almost reluctantly, and then wondered at herself.

'Thank you.' With another smile she passed both women and went out into the garden. She closed the door carefully behind her.

'Bernice,' Claris murmured.

'Ah.' Neither woman said anything for a while, and then Lydia sighed. 'I shouldn't have been rude.'

'You aren't feeling well,' Claris excused. 'Why don't you go back to bed? I can do the picnic.'

'I'm perfectly capable...'

'I know you are,' Claris agreed gently. 'And you really must know that I'm not trying to suggest anything else.' Getting to her feet, she put her arm round the housekeeper. 'Go back to bed,' she repeated softly. 'I'm perfectly capable of assembling a picnic.'

'Well, I do feel a bit—odd. Perhaps there's a bug going round.'

'Perhaps. I'll bring you up a cup of tea before we go.'

'All right.' With obvious reluctance she walked out, and Claris listened to her heavy steps as she went up the stairs.

Wearing a thoughtful expression, Claris opened the fridge to see what there was to put in sandwiches. Taking out cold meat and salad, cheese and tomato, she stood where she could see into the garden and began buttering the bread. She could only see Bernice, but she was obviously talking to *someone*. And if she opened the back door in order to hear what they were saying... Disgusted with herself, she wondered why on earth she cared. She had never yearned to overhear Adam's conversations with Arabella.

Five minutes later Adam walked in, the baby clasped in his arms. He gave her a bland smile.

'Bernice gone?' she asked quietly.

'Mmm.'

'She didn't stay long.'

'No.' Because he'd told her to leave? Knowing better than to ask, Claris got on with what she was doing.

'I thought you'd be pleased to see her,' he murmured provocatively.

'Why would I be pleased? Or even otherwise? Her visit has nothing to do with me.'

'No, but you were the one who reminded me of family obligations.' Taking one of the crusts she'd cut off, he handed it to Nathan.

'Probably because I don't have any, and I wasn't aware that Bernice was family. Pass me the pickle, will you?'

'I don't like pickle.'

'I do.'

He laughed, and obediently passed it across. 'Where's Lydia?'

'Gone back to bed. She thinks she might have picked up a bug. Or it might be the heat. I'll check on her before we go.'

'She's all right to be left?'

'I think so. She's no longer young...'

'My fault?' he asked softly.

Surprised, she swung round to face him. 'No! And don't you ever accuse her of being too old to work! Sorry,' she apologised hastily. 'Sorry.' Cross with herself for such an overreaction, she began slapping cold meat onto her buttered bread, and then halted as the startling thought struck her that maybe that was why Lydia had mentioned Adam getting married. Perhaps she *wanted* to retire? Perhaps she thought that if he did so, she could go. But go where? Facing Adam again, who was watching her with an interested expression on his face, she asked him, 'What will she do when she retires?'

'Whatever she chooses,' he said easily. 'It's been discussed, Claris.'

'And it's none of my business, is it?' she asked guiltily. 'It was just that...'

'You have a kind heart. And no relatives of your own,' he tacked on softly. 'Feeling old, Claris? Imagining yourself at her age?'

'Don't be silly,' she refuted, but it was uncomfortably close to her own thoughts in the inn. Hastily changing the subject, she asked, 'Why didn't you tell me you'd gone to see the Colonel?'

'Because nothing came of it. We were unable to find out who fired the stone.'

And so it wasn't important enough to mention? Changing tack, she asked, 'Will we still live here when the baby goes home?'

'Don't know. Do you want to live here?'

'It isn't up to me. Which cake? Fruit or chocolate?'

'Chocolate. Bernice invited me to dinner with herself and Harriet.'

'That's nice,' she commented neutrally.

'Is it?'

'Sure. How bad could it be?'

'The word "dire" springs to mind,' he drawled, and she laughed, relieved. She hadn't liked the other girl, and didn't really know why.

'You don't like her?'

'No, Claris, I didn't like her.'

'Did you tell her so?'

'Oh, I'm sure she had *some* perception. Not a great deal, perhaps, but some. She had thought it might be nice to dine *en famille*, as they say.'

'And what did you say?' she asked as she wrapped

the sandwiches in greaseproof paper and stacked them in the hamper.

'That Harriet is my aunt by marriage, not by inclination.'

Yes, she could imagine him saying it. In a very bored voice, of course. 'She's quite pretty.'

'I don't like "quite" pretty.'

'No,' she agreed, 'you like lovely. Anyway, she was too short for you,' she told him quietly. 'Kissing her would give you a crick in the neck.'

'You, on the other hand,' he said from very close behind her, 'are just the right height.'

Alarmed, she swung round to face him—and her bad eye came into contact with Nathan's waving fist. 'Ouch.' Unable to step back because of the table behind her, she moved sideways. Keeping a wary eye on the pair of them, she collected the wine and one of the meals Lydia always had prepared for the baby from the fridge, put them in the hamper and closed the lid.

'Are we ready now?' he asked mockingly.

'Almost. Just let me make Lydia a cup of tea and make sure she's all right. I'll meet you at the car,' she added hastily.

He gave a soft laugh—which she found extraordinarily alarming. What on earth was the matter with him lately? First he'd kissed her, and now he was making very odd suggestions.

Five minutes later, she climbed in beside him.

'How is she?' he asked.

'She said not to fuss. I think she's all right. I said we wouldn't be too long.'

He looked amused as he put the car into gear and

drove out. Claris turned around to check on the baby as they drove towards Winchelsea, and saw that he'd fallen asleep.

Facing forward again, her mind more on Adam's odd behaviour than anything else, she wanted very much to ask him what he was playing at, but if she did that it would give the whole thing far more importance than it warranted. 'Are you sure this picnic is a good idea?' she murmured.

'Of course it is. Didn't you know that all my ideas are to be thought excellent?'

'That doesn't mean they are.'

'No,' he agreed softly, and then he laughed, almost as though he were mocking himself.

They found a field, with a stream, wildflowers and wildlife—but no cows, and if there were nettles Claris didn't see any. They spread the blanket, set out the hamper and some of Nathan's toys, and sat down. After what seemed an eternity of silence, while they both watched the baby crawling about and rescued several daisies from being eaten, Claris started to laugh. And then found it very hard to stop. It was all so absurd, and the mockery in his eyes only made her laugh harder, which made her swollen eye hurt.

'This is so silly. What do people *do* on picnics? They can't just sit and watch the countryside for hours on end.'

'I think they play cricket and rounders,' he murmured.

She snorted. 'Did we bring a cricket bat? A ball?'

'No.'

'No,' she agreed.

'And then they have lunch,' he continued amiably, 'and then they go to sleep for half an hour, and then they go home.'

'Wow.'

'Is it too early for lunch?'

She glanced at her watch, then hastily scrambled after the baby to rescue another plant from his mouth and hauled him back to the rug. 'It's just gone eleven,' she informed him drily.

Lying back, he plucked a stalk of grass and began to chew it. Nathan promptly scrambled onto his chest and peered into his face. Drawing up his knees, he sat the baby against them, and gave him his watch to play with.

'He'll break it,' she warned.

'Doesn't matter. You aren't afraid of me, Claris, are you?' he asked softly.

Surprised, she shook her head. 'Why would I be afraid of you?'

'Nervous, then?'

'No.' Well, she *hadn't* been.

'Everyone else seems to be.'

'You can be—intimidating,' she observed. 'Are we talking about Bernice? I wouldn't have said she was nervous. She seemed very self-assured.'

'She was. I don't like people very much.'

'I know,' she agreed drily.

'You're the only person I've ever employed who answers me back.'

'And is that why I'm still here?'

'Probably. Did Bernice say anything to you?'

'No.'

'Nothing about my aunt?'

'No,' she repeated.

'Nothing about Harriet's portfolio?'

'No. Did she mention it to you?'

'Yes. She said she was worried.'

'Then it was probably Bernice who made the anonymous phone calls,' Claris observed.

'Perhaps. I don't like being agreed with all the time. Or dictated to,' he tacked on softly.

Foolish Bernice, she thought, if that was what she'd done.

'But then, I can't imagine you being dictated to either.'

'Children's homes don't allow for—meekness,' Claris said. 'If you don't fight, you go under. I don't entirely understand where this conversation is going. You think Bernice tried to dictate to me?'

'No. How old were you when you went into the home?'

'A few weeks.' She'd told Mrs Staple Smythe her family home was in Leicester, and not to ask if her parents were married. The truth of the matter was she had no idea who her parents were, let alone if they'd been married. And her family home *was* in Leicester. The occupants of the children's home were the only family she had. As far as she knew.

Turning his head, Adam stared at her profile. Her dark glasses hid the worst of the damage to her eye, but he could still see the butterfly tapes across her cheekbone. 'It will leave a scar,' he commented softly.

With a small smile, she put up a hand to gently touch the wound. 'Not much of one. Perhaps it will make me interesting.'

'You're already interesting.'

A slight feeling of wrongness inside, a small feeling of alarm, she quipped, 'Compliments, Adam?'

'Why not? No,' he reproved gently, and Claris turned to see him remove his watch from Nathan's mouth.

Adam turned to meet her eyes. 'Did no one want to adopt you?'

'No. I was a sickly baby with the added disadvantage of ginger hair. I was fostered out once or twice, but I was a bit—disruptive.'

He smiled. 'Good for you.' Returning his attention to the baby, he handed him a plastic shape which promptly went into his mouth. 'I don't know if he's hungry or just teething.'

'Both, I expect. It's time for his lunch anyway.'

He shouldn't have kissed her, he thought with wry self-mockery as he watched her unpack the baby's lunch. It had made her wary, and that wasn't what he wanted at all. Not that he was entirely sure *what* he wanted. He only knew that the delightful Miss Newman was seriously disrupting the calm waters of his normally agreeable existence. A new experience for him. As was the baby. They had both given him thoughts he didn't normally have.

Claris lifted Nathan to sit in front of her, and Adam watched her fit his bib. She had nice hands: long-fingered, elegant. She wasn't in the least pretty, but she had an appeal that went far beyond it. And she was very aware of him watching her.

'Why did you invite me?' she asked quietly.

He smiled. 'You aren't supposed to ask.'

'Just be grateful for the attention?' she asked drily.

He laughed. '*That* was why.' Lying back, he stared up at the sky. 'What does my aunt want?'

'For you to marry,' she said naughtily. 'She thinks single gentlemen who play the field are dangerous. No,' she reproved Nathan, 'eat it nicely—and give me back the spoon. Thank you.'

'Dangerous to whom?'

'Her niece?' she guessed, and then laughed. 'I don't know, Adam. Really. She fired questions at me like bullets from a gun, asked if the baby was yours, and told me that Wentsham morals were very upright.'

'Are they giving you a hard time?'

'How can they give me a hard time?' she quipped. 'I'm not allowed into the village. You said so. There's a good boy.' Wiping Nathan's mouth, she put the lid back on the pot, and put it, along with the spoon, back in the polythene bag. Reaching for his bottle, she hauled him onto her lap and began to give it to him. She had a small smile on her face, a smile she was quite unaware of. She stared down at the serene face below hers. 'I shan't want to give him back,' she said softly. 'Jenny must miss him desperately.'

'Yes,' he agreed. 'But we decided that it might upset him too much to see his parents and then to be taken away again. You'd like them.'

She merely smiled.

The baby's eyes began to close, and her smile softened. 'I think I want a baby of my own,' she said without thinking.

'Any time,' he said softly, not only surprising himself, but her as well. 'I wouldn't sack you,' he added quickly, as though that was what he'd meant. 'But I would prefer you to be married. For you to do it—properly.'

'Yes, unmarried mothers aren't much liked in Wentsham,' she agreed with a little twinkle in her eye. 'The doctor asked me out,' she added casually.

'Did he?' he asked neutrally.

'Yes.'

'And shall you go?'

'I might.'

But I don't want you to, he thought. 'What's he like?'

'Amiable,' she murmured. And then she smiled, gave him a teasing sideways glance. 'Lacking in judgement?'

She had said it as a joke, expecting him to laugh, but for some reason he didn't find it at all amusing. Changing the subject, he asked abruptly. 'Is he asleep?'

'Almost.'

Sitting up, reaching for the baby's blanket, he folded it and placed it in the shade. 'Here, I'll put him down.' Reaching across, he gently lifted him and placed him on the blanket.

Unsettled by Adam's behaviour, she put the cap on the bottle and slowly set out their picnic. It didn't look very inspiring. Neither did she feel very hungry. The wine was warm, the bread beginning to curl, and the cake looked soggy. Not Adam's scene at all. But then, what was Adam's scene? A few days ago she would have said she knew very well. Today, she didn't.

As soon as they'd eaten she made the excuse that they ought to go, that she didn't want to leave Lydia for too long. Adam didn't demur. Perhaps she'd bored him again. The thought depressed her.

A strange, unsettling day, she thought as they drove home. Adam was silent, his earlier humour forgotten. And why on earth had she said that about a baby? She had no intention of having a baby. No yet, anyway. And Adam had been—odd. Better if they stuck to a business relationship. Perhaps it was living in close proximity. She might have done better to have got herself rooms nearby, just come in every day as she had in London.

'Are you going to the hospital today?' she asked as they pulled into the drive.

'Maybe later. I seem to have developed Lydia's headache.' He sounded as though he were mocking himself.

She had one too. With a funny little sigh, she unstrapped the baby whilst Adam collected the picnic things and led the way inside. Lydia was obviously still in her room.

Worried, Claris handed the baby to Adam and walked upstairs. She tapped lightly on the housekeeper's door, and gently opened it when there was no answer. Lydia was lying on her bed. A scarf was draped across her eyes and the curtains were drawn.

'Lydia?' Claris called softly, and the housekeeper turned her head towards her. Walking across to the bed, she asked worriedly, 'Are you all right?'

'No,' she denied almost crossly as she removed the scarf. 'I feel terrible. Claris, I *ache*. Maybe I ate something that didn't agree with me. Even my eyes hurt.'

'Have you taken anything?'

'Aspirins.'

Perching on the edge of the mattress, she picked up Lydia's hand, and that was when she saw the rash. 'I'm going to call the doctor,' she announced.

'No.'

'Yes.' Patting Lydia's hand in rough comfort, she went quickly downstairs. Adam was in the lounge with the baby.

'How is she?'

'Not too good. Her eyes ache and she has a rash. I'm going to call the doctor. Do you have the number for the clinic?'

'In the phone book on the hall table.'

She hurried out, quickly dialled, and waited whilst the call was transferred to the doctor's home. She explained, and thanked him when he said he'd be right out.

'He's on his way,' she told Adam as she walked back into the lounge. Funny, her eyes ached as well. Squinting slightly, she turned her back on the window, and Adam caught her arm as she passed his chair.

He examined it for any rash, and, finding none, gave it back to her. 'Just testing,' he said humorously. 'How do you feel?'

'All right,' she murmured dubiously. 'A bit achy.'

'Then I suggest you sit down. Do you want anything? A cup of tea? Some aspirins?'

She shook her head, then winced. Sitting on the sofa, she stared at her arms. They were as clear as they usually were. 'Perhaps Lydia has an allergy.'

'Stop speculating and wait for the doctor. I'll go and see how she is.'

She nodded.

'Cheer up,' he said kindly. 'I'm sure it's nothing much.'

'I hope not,' she retorted. 'I'm not very good at cooking.'

He laughed. So did the doctor when he came down from visiting Lydia.

'I don't find it *funny*, Doctor,' she said acerbically.

'No. Sorry,' he apologised. 'I really shouldn't laugh.' He checked her eyes, her throat, her pulse, her skin and, a smile still in his eyes, he pronounced softly, 'You seem to have escaped.'

'Escaped *what*?'

'Measles.'

CHAPTER FIVE

'*MEASLES*?' she exclaimed in disbelief. 'Lydia has *measles*?'

'Yes.' Seating himself on the sofa, Dr Markham patted the cushion beside him.

Ignoring the gesture, Claris perched on the arm of the chair. 'Where on earth would she have caught measles? She hasn't been anywhere!'

He glanced at the baby and asked quietly, 'Has he had his MMR vaccine recently?'

'MMR?'

'Measles, mumps and rubella,' he explained.

'I don't know. I could find out. But you surely can't catch it from a vaccination, can you?'

'You can from a dirty nappy. Which is no doubt why the elegant Adam hasn't caught it,' he added.

'I haven't caught it either,' she pointed out. 'And Adam *does* change his nappy,' she added defensively, and then wondered at her attitude. Why did she need to defend him, for goodness' sake?

'Does he?' he asked in obvious astonishment, 'Good Lord.'

'He's very good with the baby!'

The doctor smiled. 'Trod on your toes, did I?'

'No. It's just... Well, he's not the way people think he is.' Yes, he is, she told herself disgustedly. Mostly, anyway. But he did help out with the baby. In fact, he was very good with him, which had surprised her.

The fact that he didn't *treat* him like a baby was beside the point, and it didn't seem to bother Nathan at all. Admittedly most of the changing and dressing was done by Lydia and herself, but Adam *had* changed him on occasion, and certainly he bathed him and played with him. 'I certainly didn't know you could catch measles from a nappy. Will she be all right?

'Should be.'

'*Should* be? What on earth does that mean?'

He smiled again. 'Exactly what it says. Plenty of liquids, paracetamol for the pain, and if her eyes hurt make sure she stays out of direct light. She should be better in a few days. Then we can have our date,' he added softly. 'How's the eye?'

'It's fine.' Still worried, still examining his face, she asked, 'Lydia's really all right? I always thought measles was dangerous in an adult.'

'Not necessarily. Measles *can* affect the eyes, but there's no sign that it's done so. Ring me if she gets worse, although I don't anticipate any problems. He's a nice little chap, isn't he?' he added, nodding towards the baby, who was busily playing with his bricks.

'Yes.'

'And you're a nice lady. Give me a ring when you're less harrassed. You look like someone I could grow fond of.' Getting to his feet, he gave a small flap of his hand and walked out.

Someone he could grow *fond* of? That had a nice ring to it. Although he'd been rather too casual about the measles for her liking. She was quite sure she had read that it could be dangerous.

Adam appeared moments later, and she asked quietly, 'How is she?'

'Intent on getting up.'

She opened her mouth to protest, then closed it when he gave her a bland smile.

'Do we have any paracetamol?' he asked.

'There should be some in the kitchen cabinet.'

He nodded. 'Do you want any?'

She shook her head.

'All right, just let me see to Lydia, and then I'll get Nathan's tea. What would you like for dinner?'

Astonished, she just stared at him.

'You think me incapable?'

'No, not *incapable*.'

'Just abominably selfish?' he queried. 'Then you'd best make the most of my offer, hadn't you? I doubt it will last,' he added laconically as he strolled out, and then he gave a wry smile. Adam, who never put himself out for anyone, had now promoted himself to being in charge of the sick room. The odd thing was, he didn't seem to mind.

Adam fed the baby, bathed him and put him to bed. Still somewhat amused by his own behaviour, he made a salad for Lydia, Claris and himself, loaded the dishwasher, and then rang the hospital.

Walking into the lounge to find Claris with her feet up on the sofa, he smiled. 'The baby had his injection the day before the accident,' he told her quietly. 'Don't get up; you can listen equally well lying down.' When she'd subsided, he walked across to the armchair and sat facing her. 'I asked the nurse to ask the grandparents, and told them that I wouldn't be in for a few days. Head still ache?'

'A bit. Too much sun, I expect.'

'Mmm,' he agreed blandly. 'What did the good doctor have to say?'

'Nothing much, just to ring him when I was feeling better.'

'Ah, yes, the date.'

'Stop being derisive,' she scolded tiredly. 'He thinks I'm a nice lady.'

'So do I.'

She snorted, trying not to believe it, trying not to care. Straightening, she swung her legs to the floor. 'I'm going to bed.' It seemed to have been a very long day. 'Goodnight, Adam.'

Eyes full of amusement, he asked softly, 'Need any help?'

'No, thank you.'

The stairs seemed like a mountain, the landing along to her room a mile. Her head hurt, and so did her back, but she didn't have measles. The doctor had said so. And he should know, shouldn't he? Thankfully closing her bedroom door, she stripped off and tumbled into bed. She would not think about Adam, or the doctor, or anything else. Tomorrow everything would be back to normal.

When she woke in the morning, she felt better. Lydia felt worse. Walking in to the housekeeper's room before going downstairs, Claris gave her a sympathetic smile. 'How do you feel?'

'Old.'

Claris laughed. 'Do you need anything?'

'No, Adam seems to have risen rather magnificently to the occasion. He brought me my breakfast earlier. How do *you* feel?'

'Me? I'm fine.'

'Your eye looks better. Not so swollen.'

'No.'

'I'll get up later.'

'You will not!' Claris ordered. 'You're to stay in bed.'

'But I need to go into the town.'

'*I* will go into the town. Make a list. I'll come back and see you when I've had my breakfast. Call if you need anything.' Closing the door, Claris went down to the kitchen and found it empty. Retreating along the hall, she pushed open the study door and peeked inside. Empty. Trying the lounge, much to her astonishment, she found Adam and Colonel Davenport drinking coffee. Nathan was on the floor playing with an empty box.

Adam smiled at her. 'How do you feel?'

'I'm fine, thank you. Good morning, Colonel.'

He got gallantly to his feet and smiled at her. 'Morning. Just having a chat with young Adam here. Eye looks nasty,' he commented. 'As if you didn't have enough to worry about. Such nonsense. Don't have anything to do with them myself. Best. Don't get involved is my motto.'

'And that from a man who was just trying to persuade me to get involved in vandalism?' Adam murmured drily.

The Colonel laughed. 'That's different.'

'Of course it is.'

Time for her to retreat, Claris decided, before Adam could recall the Colonel's earlier words. 'I'll, um, leave you to it, then.' Not even asking whether Adam wanted her to take the baby, she backed out and went along to the kitchen to make herself toast and coffee.

Adam appeared when she had nearly finished, Nathan crawling behind him.

'Who doesn't the Colonel have anything to do with?' he asked quietly.

She looked at him, then looked quickly away. 'It's not important.'

'Who?' he repeated.

And he would stand there all day if necessary, wouldn't he? Until she answered him. 'You really don't want to be bothered with it, Adam.'

'But I do, Miss Newman. I do.'

She sighed, watched as Nathan crawled towards the washing machine. He liked the washing machine. That boy was going to be a mechanic, she decided. He opened the outer wooden door, opened the glass porthole and put his head inside. Retreating, he closed the door and peered through the glass. He would spend hours doing that if anyone let him.

His eyes also on the baby, Adam prompted quietly, 'Claris?' When she didn't immediately answer him, he continued thoughtfully, 'Mrs Staple Smythe I know about, but the Colonel said "them" not "her". Who was he talking about? Who isn't speaking to you, Claris?'

'The village,' she muttered as she continued to watch Nathan. Head back in the washing machine, he was slowly revolving the drum with one chubby hand.

'The *whole* village?'

'With the exception of the Colonel, yes.'

'Why?'

'Don't know.'

'Yes, you do.'

She sighed again and turned to look at him. 'It isn't a problem. You pay me to deal with things. I'm dealing with it.'

'How?'

'Adam,' she protested, beginning to feel cross.

'Tell me.'

'No. It's much better if I don't.' Finishing her coffee, she got up to put her empty cup in the sink. Assuming that Adam was going to look after Nathan, she attempted to walk past him. He caught her arm to halt her.

'I need to go into Rye for Lydia.'

'Rye isn't going anywhere.' Eyes on her mutinous face, and the glory of her bruised eye, he waited.

'I don't know why,' she denied. 'Not for sure.'

'Then tell me what you suspect.'

'That they want me to leave.'

'Why?'

'I don't *know*! Because I'm not suitable, because… Adam, it's not important!'

'It is to me.'

'Why?' she demanded. 'Why is it important? You've never become involved before! I deal with things! It's what I'm for! And being ignored by a bunch of silly women doesn't bother me at all!' Pulling her arm free, she stalked upstairs.

Collecting Lydia's list, she went into her own room to get her bag and car keys, and then went back down. Adam was waiting for her in the hall.

'Do you want me to take Nathan?'

'He shook his head.

'Then I'll see you later.' Brushing past him, she headed for the side door.

'Claris?'

Halting, she waited.

'Can you see properly to drive?'

'Yes.'

'Then drive safely—I can hardly complain about your independence when that's exactly what I wanted, can I?' he added softly.

'No,' she agreed. 'I won't be long. Is there anything you need?'

He was silent for a moment, and then he gave a little chuckle. 'A paddling pool?'

She did turn then, and he smiled at her.

'For Nathan.'

She smiled back, finally relaxed. 'OK. I'll see you later.' Her small smile still in place, she walked out to the old stable block. She backed her car out and then opened all the windows to create a breeze before heading for the town.

Driving through the newish housing estate, such a stark contrast to Wentsham itself, she wondered with a wry smile how much opposition had been put up to its being built. Quite a lot, she would have imagined. Mrs Staple Smythe would have been in her element. When she got stuck behind a tractor, she had ample time to look around her. A group of young boys were hanging around an old tree. They appeared to be throwing stones up into the branches. It was a bit early for conkers, she would have thought. Removing her sunglasses in order to see better, just in *case* they were up to something they shouldn't be, she chuckled when they all turned to look at her. Such *innocence* on their young faces! She thought she saw one of the boys thrust a catapult behind his back. She'd had no intention of admonishing them, or asking what they were doing, but if a *catapult* was involved... She halted the car, but wasn't entirely surprised when they fled.

Hmm, might be worth asking the Colonel if he knew who they were. Not that she wished to get anyone into trouble, and boys, as they said, would be boys, but if it *had* been a catapult it might be worth getting it confiscated before someone else got hurt.

She drove on into the town, still slowly until the tractor turned off and parked down by the Quay. She walked along to the High Street, where she got everything on Lydia's list; it was the paddling pool that gave her problems. She eventually tracked one down in the hardware shop near the post office.

Hot, sticky and overloaded, she struggled back to the car, and had just finished putting everything into the boot when she saw Bernice. Unfortunately, Bernice also saw her.

'Hello,' the other girl greeted her with a warm smile. 'How's the eye? I heard what happened.'

'It's fine, thank you.'

'Why not come and have a coffee with me? You look as though you could do with one.'

Taken by surprise, because for some reason she hadn't expected *friendship*, Claris demurred, 'Oh, I don't think so. It's very kind of you, but really I have to get back.'

'Oh, come on, it won't take long. Harriet's out and

I'm bored.' Tucking her arm into Claris's, Bernice urged her back towards the town. 'It isn't far; she has a little house up by the church. You wouldn't *believe* the gossip that's going round about you and Adam,' she confided with a laugh as they walked up the hill.

'Oh, I would,' Claris said drily, as she wondered if she hadn't rather badly misjudged the other girl.

'But then, a single *and* good-looking male tends to get people talking.'

'Not to say wealthy,' Claris agreed softly.

Bernice laughed.

At least she hadn't pretended not to know, Claris thought, which was something in her favour.

'And I know he *is* single—well, unattached emotionally,' she qualified, 'because he said so.'

Claris very much doubted it. Adam never told anyone anything.

'And that makes him fair game, doesn't it?' Bernice smiled.

'For you?' Claris asked softly.

'Of course for me. And here we are.' Fitting her key in the front door of the tiny house opposite the church, she led Claris inside. 'Make yourself at home,' she ordered, 'I'll go and make the coffee. Adam said you were clever,' she called as Claris settled herself on the small settee.

'Did he?' she asked noncommittally. In what context? Glancing round at the small, beautifully appointed room, she stared at the framed photographs on the mantelpiece. Harriet's late husband? Adam's uncle? Getting up to have a look, she tried to find a resemblance to her employer, and couldn't. He looked a severe man—but then, Adam could look pretty severe when he chose.

'Uncle George,' Bernice murmured from behind her. 'Very moral. Come and have your coffee.'

Returning to the settee, Claris watched Bernice settle herself opposite.

'You work for him, don't you?' she asked, with a rather teasing smile. 'I'm afraid I rather naughtily peeped into the office when I came looking for Adam at the Manor. There were two desks.'

'Mmm,' Claris agreed.

'So,' she continued, 'if you work for him, and if you're as clever as Adam seems to think—because he wouldn't employ you if you weren't, and I know he *does* employ you because a woman in the village was asked by a rather beautiful young woman for directions…'

Arabella. 'And this woman asked her who I was,' Claris stated fatalistically. And naturally Arabella would have answered.

Bernice laughed. 'People are so *nosy*, aren't they?'

'Yes. You were saying?'

'That I wondered if you would look over my little list of investments. Hang on a minute.' Getting up, she hurried away, and came back two minutes later holding a piece of paper which she placed on the coffee table in front of Claris.

'*Your* investments?'

'Yes.'

Staring at the other girl, making no attempt to pick up the piece of paper, Claris stated quietly, 'Harriet's investments.'

'Oh, all right! Harriet's investments!'

'It was you who made the anonymous phone calls.'

Bernice looked down, gave a small smile, then shrugged. 'Yes, it was me,' she agreed. 'Harriet is the only close relative I have. I was worried about her. Am still worried.'

Eyes never wavering, Claris mused thoughtfully, 'Worried she won't have anything to leave you when she dies?'

'No!' Bernice protested. 'No, oh, you can't think that!'

'Of course I can think it,' Claris argued softly. 'It doesn't necessarily make it *true*…'

'It isn't, Claris. I promise you it isn't.'

Claris didn't know if she believed her.

'All you have to do is look at it,' she begged. 'What harm could it do?'

'Cause trouble?' Claris said promptly. 'If Harriet knows nothing about this…'

'She won't *ask*,' Bernice said crossly. 'She is so…'

'Private? I think I'd better go.' Picking up her coffee, she quickly drank it and got to her feet.

'Take the paper anyway,' Bernice persuaded her. 'And if you won't look at it, ask Adam. He *is* her nephew.'

And much good that would do anyone. Claris gave a brief laugh, but didn't explain why she had done so. Anyway, she seemed to remember that Adam had said that Bernice already *had* asked him.

'Thanks for the drink,' she murmured politely. 'No, don't get up; I can see myself out.' Looping her bag over her shoulder, she walked into the hall.

Bernice got up anyway, and followed her to the

front door. 'Don't be angry with me,' she begged as Claris stepped out and turned to say goodbye.

'I'm not angry,' she denied mildly. 'I'll see you around, I expect. Bye.'

Walking down the hill and back to her car, face thoughtful, Claris suddenly laughed. She'd just been used, hadn't she? Or had she? Certainly it had been opportunistic. There was no doubt, of course, that Bernice was worried. But genuinely worried for Harriet—or for herself? Claris didn't know.

Rummaging in her bag for her keys, she came across a folded piece of paper. Opening it, she stared at it, and then put it back. The quickness of the hand had deceived the eye. Bernice had obviously slipped it into her bag at the front door.

Opening the car, she climbed inside and hastily wound down both windows and opened the roof. It was like a sauna. So, she decided, as she drove slowly out of the car park, not only did she have Mrs SS and the villagers to look out for, but Bernice—and Harriet, if she ever found out what her niece had done. Dismissing it, too hot to care at the moment, she went home—to find a car blocking the driveway.

Resignedly parking behind it, she unloaded the shopping, trudged up to the side gate, and carried it indoors. She wondered if anyone was watching. Well, if they were, they'd get no satisfaction from the expression on her face. If they were hoping for a temper tantrum, they were going to be disappointed.

When she'd put the shopping away in the kitchen, she carried the paddling pool along to the study and handed it to a frowning Adam.

'Problems?' she asked lightly.

'Mmm? No, not really, just thinking about something. You were a long time.'

She smiled. 'Bernice invited me in for coffee. The secret's out, I'm afraid.'

'What secret?'

His mind obviously still on what was bugging him, she murmured, 'The secret of our relationship. Arabella asked for directions in the village.'

He blinked, focused on her properly, and then smiled. 'Ah.'

'So,' she continued, 'I imagine the latest story is that the baby is mine, because Arabella didn't know that he wasn't, but you magnanimously allow me to work for you because I'm clever...'

'And my reputation is saved because it has been seen that I have a glamorous girlfriend.'

'And I have a problem.'

'What sort of problem?'

'Moral, I think. Where's Nathan?'

'Having a nap.'

She nodded. Taking the piece of paper from her bag, she handed it to him. 'Don't open it for a minute,' she instructed, and explained all that had happened. 'So you see,' she added, 'I don't know whether to look at it or throw it away. If your aunt *is* being cheated, then do I have a duty to tell her? If she isn't, do I keep quiet? And I can't quite make up my mind about Bernice.'

'Then leave it with me.'

'Yes?'

'Don't look so surprised,' he reproved drily.

'Sorry,' she laughed. Glad that everything seemed

back to normal between them, she turned away. 'I'm going to have a shower. I'm hot!'

Sticking her head into Lydia's room on her way, she smiled. 'How are you feeling?'

'Much better. Baby still asleep?'

'I'm just going to check.'

Lydia nodded. 'What on earth are we going to do when he's gone?' she asked quietly.

'Miss him,' Claris said soberly. 'The grandparents will be being discharged soon.'

'And they will, naturally, want him to stay with them.'

'Yes.'

Lydia gave a deep sigh, and forced a smile. 'Did you get everything?'

'Yes, and, Nathan permitting, I'm going to have a shower.'

'OK.'

Ten minutes later she made another check on the baby, to find him still fast asleep, and lingered a moment to stare down at him. Lydia was right. What on earth were they going to do without him? He had become so much a part of their lives. Perhaps the grandparents could come here to convalesce... But it would only delay the inevitable, wouldn't it?

Feeling depressed, she went downstairs. Having asked Adam if he wanted a sandwich, she made them both one, and returned to the study.

As she settled herself at her desk, he asked quietly, 'Have you ever heard of business angels?'

'Vaguely. Something to do with the gap between bank loans and venture capital, aren't they?'

'Mmm. Sums in between can be surprisingly dif-

ficult to obtain unless you can find a business angel
willing to back you.'

'The way you did with Mark and Sara?'

'Yes, although I really would prefer not to call myself a business angel,' he derided, with an expression
of distaste that made her laugh. 'The concept isn't
new, of course,' he continued, 'and normally, as you
know, I find my own investment opportunities.
However, I've been approached by an investment broker who wants to marry up suitable growing firms
with private backers.'

'For an equity stake?'

'Mmm. Risk in exchange for a possible high return.'

'Much what you're doing anyway.'

'Except I wouldn't have to go looking. He's send-
ing me some literature over by courier—I'd like you
to look at it if you will.'

'Sure.'

Picking up the piece of paper she had given him,
still folded, he held it for a moment between finger
and thumb, and then deliberately tore it in half. 'If
Harriet wants me to look at her investments, she can
ask me herself and I will do so. This is an invasion
of privacy.'

She nodded. Still watching him, her mind still really on Nathan, and what his departure would mean,
she murmured, 'Adam? I've been thinking.'

'Dangerous.'

She smiled. 'Do you know what Jenny's parents'
plans are when they're released from the hospital?
They won't *immediately* be able to look after the
baby, will they?'

'No, they'll need to convalesce.'

'Yes, and so I was thinking—well, if it's within the next few weeks, as you seem to think, why don't you invite them to stay here?'

He gave her a long, rather dry look. 'I don't have enough to do?' he asked interestedly.

'No! Listen, let me finish. You could then go off and do your endurance rally...'

'Trying to get rid of me, Miss Newman?'

'No,' she denied more seriously. 'but it was something you really wanted to do, wasn't it?'

Swivelling his chair to fully face her, he stared at her for some moments in silence, and then said quietly, 'What a very strange girl you are.'

'Am I?' she asked in surprise. 'Why?'

'Because you are so totally unselfish.'

'No, I'm not,' she denied, embarrassed. 'In fact, quite the reverse. I was trying to hang onto the baby for a little bit longer,' she confessed. 'And there's nothing major coming up,' she continued quickly. 'Nothing that I, or your London office can't deal with. You won't exactly be uncontactable, will you? I mean, I know you'd have to discuss it with Lydia, because although I can help out with cleaning and suchlike, the bulk of the cooking will land on her. Think about it anyway.' Feeling awkward at the way he continued to stare at her, almost wishing she hadn't mentioned it, she quickly turned away and switched on her computer.

'Thank you,' he said quietly.

'For what?' she asked, without looking at him.

'Being you.' Getting to his feet, he added in the bland voice that usually made her smile, 'I think I'll go and blow up the paddling pool.' Picking it up, he carried it out into the garden.

Face thoughtful, she called up the file she wanted. He had spoken almost as though no one ever did anything for him without an ulterior motive, and yet that couldn't be true. And she hadn't been being unselfish.

With a funny little sigh, she began altering the report he would need for Thursday's board meeting to incorporate the few changes he'd made. After printing out several copies, she bound them and left them on his desk before ringing their young computer expert to find out how he was doing.

When Nathan woke up, Adam took him out into the garden to play in his paddling pool. She could hear splashes and shrieks, Adam's laugher, and she smiled. They really were going to miss him so much when he left. And if she didn't get herself a social life she was going to turn into a cabbage. Thinking about it for only a moment, she finally picked up the phone and rang the doctor.

Her evening out with him wasn't a great success. Her fault, probably. She kept remembering Adam's face when she'd left. Mocking, derisive—and something else. Chris didn't seem entirely comfortable either. Sitting in a small pub on the outskirts of Rye, they both toyed with their drinks.

'I'm sorry,' she apologised awkwardly. 'I'm not being very good company, am I?'

'Why did you come?' he asked.

'Because you asked me?' she quipped, and then apologised. 'Sorry. It's been an unsettling couple of days.'

'Are you in love with him?' he asked quietly.

'Sorry?'

'Adam Turmaine.'

'No, of course I'm not in love with him!' she denied quickly.

'Of course?' he asked wryly.

'Yes. I work for him.'

'I know.'

Concerned, wary, she asked, 'Why on earth would you think I was in love with him?'

He shrugged.

'Has he said something?'

'No,' he denied. 'When would he have had any chance to say anything?'

'He let you in, and you were talking together before I came down.'

'Not about anything important. Come on, I'll take you home.'

Not unwilling, she collected her bag. He parked the car in the lane and walked with her to the side door. 'Don't take the butterfly tapes off until Friday, will you?' he cautioned. 'Goodnight, Claris.' Dropping a light kiss on her cheek, he walked away. She waited until she heard his car start up before going in. She wasn't sure why.

Adam was just coming out of the lounge as she closed the door. He looked surprised, or pretended to be.

'You're early.'

'Yes,' she agreed quietly.

'Not entirely successful?' he asked wryly.

'No. Did you say anything to him?'

'Say anything?' he asked, at his most bland.

Giving him a look of disgust, she headed for the stairs. 'Goodnight, Adam,' she said firmly.

'Never go to bed in a temper,' he reproved softly. 'Come on, I'll make you a nightcap.' Without waiting for an answer, he returned to the lounge.

She wasn't in a temper. She just felt a bit—empty. Chris Markham had obviously decided that she was no longer a lady he could like. Not that she could blame him, and she didn't know *why* she had been so quiet. Not really.

Slowly following after Adam, she saw that he hadn't switched on the lights, and the French doors stood wide open. Tossing her bag onto the sofa she went to stare into the garden.

'What went wrong?' he asked as he brought their drinks across and handed her hers.

'I don't know.' Uncomfortable at being so close to him, although heaven knew why, she stepped outside. 'He seemed to think I was in love with you.' And she wasn't. Attracted, yes, but not in love.

'Now why would he think that?'

'I don't know.' Aware of him leaning in the doorway behind her, she stared fixedly at the old apple tree that was swaying gently in the welcome breeze. She felt a bit peculiar, sort of stifled and—panicky? How foolish. Moving further out, she perched on the low wall that surrounded the small flagstoned terrace. Closing her eyes, she let the breeze wash over her face.

He joined her. Resting his forearms across his parted knees, with his drink held between them, he asked quietly, 'Have you ever been in love, Claris?'

'No.' A week ago she would have told him to mind his own business.

'So you have no idea what it feels like.'

'No.' Why did her voice sound so strangled? Why did she feel so weak? This was Adam, she kept telling herself. She could cope with Adam. She'd always coped with him. Always managed to stifle her feelings. So why not now? It must be the night air. She should go in. As she lurched to her feet her hip touched his shoulder, and she found she couldn't move. He slowly stood, gently took her glass from her hand and put both his and hers on the low wall. He seemed to be being careful, she thought in bewilderment.

'Adam...'

He touched his fingers to her mouth, and she shook.

'I'm not in love with you,' she said in a determined little voice.

'I know,' he agreed gently.

Surprised, she jerked her head round to look into his face.

'Yet,' he added, even more softly.

'What?'

'Yet,' he repeated. 'Did he kiss you goodnight?'

'It's none of your business!' she said in outrage. 'Did I ever ask you about kissing Arabella?'

He gave a small smile. 'That's because you weren't interested. Then.'

'Neither am I interested now! And this is a ridiculous conversation. I'm going to bed.' She took one step forward and he put out his arm to prevent her.

She made the mistake of looking at him. His eyes looked almost black in this light.

'Kiss me goodnight,' he persuaded softly.

'No!' she denied in horror.

'Yes.'

With a very strange feeling in her tummy, and still staring at him, almost frightened, she pleaded, 'Why?'

'Because I don't want you going to bed with the taste of the good doctor on your mouth.'

Before she could articulate a reply, think, act, he leaned forward to press a gentle kiss on her parted lips. And it was gentle, so very gentle, almost whisper-soft, and his body was warm, pliant, as he gathered her against him and deepened the kiss.

Her eyes fell closed, as though they had no will of their own, and she could feel her heart beating, so hard, so fast. Her arms hung limply by her sides, like a doll.

He moved his mouth a fraction, not far, she could still feel his breath on her face, and she slowly opened her eyes.

'Nice?' he asked softly.

Her answer was inarticulate, and he smiled. 'You look a trifle dazed, Miss Newman.'

The little sound she made in the back of her throat could have meant anything.

Moving his hands from her back, he framed her face, stared down at her, then gently threaded his fingers into her thick hair so that the tips touched her nape, and she shivered.

'You didn't come out to play in the pool this afternoon,' he reproved softly.

'I was reading the literature from the investment broker.' And taking in not a word of it. 'Anyway,' she defended, 'you didn't ask me.'

'No, but I was thinking about you, about your very generous offer.'

'Easy to be generous in someone else's house,' she pointed out, but her mind wasn't on anything they were talking about.

'Put your arms round me,' he ordered gently.

Frightened, wary, she just stared at him.

'Please?'

With another inarticulate little sound in the back of her throat, she did so, mindlessly obedient. This is Adam, she repeated to herself. Adam. Spoilt, rich, acerbic. Attractive. Devastatingly so. 'Is this how you behaved with Arabella?' she whispered. She hadn't meant to ask that.

'No, this is how I behave with you.' Bending his head again, he captured her mouth, and this time his kiss was electrifying. Her response wasn't even an option. She couldn't help but respond.

With her eyes closed, her hands groping for his shoulderblades, she pressed closer, refusing to think about where this was leading. Tomorrow there would be questions. Tomorrow she would need answers. But for now... She'd never been kissed like this, never been held like this, never felt like this, and minutes, hours, days later, when he gently, almost reluctantly, lifted his mouth, she opened dazed eyes to stare at him. His breathing was slightly accelerated. Hers was erratic.

Moving her hands to his chest, his shirt-collar, she grasped it as though it was a lifeline and he slid his own arms to her back. They stared at each other for long moments in silence, and then she licked her lips, swallowed. 'Why are you doing this to me, Adam?'

she asked huskily. 'I never imagined you would kiss me,' she continued, without waiting for his answer. 'Not once. Ever.' Unaware of what she was doing, she began to rub one palm up and down his chest. 'Not once,' she repeated.

'I know. A new experience for me.'

'And is that why? Because I never showed any interest?'

'At first, maybe. You began to intrigue me.'

'I didn't mean to.'

He gave a small, amused smile. 'Do you think I don't know that? I found myself watching you a great deal more often than I wanted to.'

'It was only a few days ago, in the Smuggler's Inn, that I bored you.'

'You never bore me,' he denied, still holding her within the circle of his arms.

'You wanted to leave.'

'I wanted to think,' he corrected, and then he smiled, wry and self-mocking. 'The picnic was supposed to be an opportunity to get to know each other better.'

'You worried me that day,' she confessed.

'I know.'

Daringly, almost awed by her behaviour, she slipped one hand up to touch his jaw, and then his mouth. She gazed at her fingers, liking the feel of his skin against them, the little shiver of awareness it gave her. She asked huskily, 'What happens now?'

Again that wry, self-mocking smile. 'I don't know.'

'You don't want to take me to bed?'

'Oh, yes—but I'm not going to.'

Disappointed, relieved, she told him firmly, 'I wouldn't have let you.'

'Good.'

She gave a weak smile and stared into his eyes. 'I feel very strange.'

'So do I. Say goodnight.'

'Now?' she asked in astonishment.

'Now.'

Searching his eyes, his face, his mouth, the mouth that had so recently touched hers, she whispered softly, 'Goodnight.' And then she kissed him, just once, briefly, almost fiercely, and released herself. She felt a deep, strange, almost welcome ache inside, and walked quickly away. Reaching the French doors, she halted, and looked back.

'The doctor didn't kiss me goodnight,' she told him quietly.

He laughed. 'I know.'

'How? How do you know? Because you were watching?'

'No. Go away.'

She remained where she was for a few seconds longer, and then slipped inside. If he hadn't been watching, how had he known?

She didn't immediately get ready for bed. How could she go to bed? Pushing her bedroom windows wide, she leaned her arms on the sill and stared out. Her room was at the side of the house and so she couldn't see the terrace from here, but she could imagine him still standing where she had left him. She felt odd, and happy, and somewhat bewildered. *Yet*, he had said. Would she one day be in love with him? She'd had no thought of it, had never allowed herself to think of it—because he wasn't for her. He liked his women beautiful... So why had he kissed her?

Troubled, disturbed, she wished she knew what had been in his mind. How would she have any idea what love felt like, he had said, if she'd never been in love? She had *imagined* what it might be like, had been very attracted once or twice, had a brief affair... But with Adam? No, she couldn't conceive of that. Adam was—well, Adam. Elegant, assured, and he only ever went out with beautiful, suitable women. She wasn't beautiful, and she had no idea if she was suitable. The whole thing seemed totally inconceivable. And yet he had kissed her. And she had responded. Had enjoyed the feel of his warm body against her own. Feeling suddenly hot, little erotic thoughts burgeoning, she hastily suppressed them and stripped off her dress. Standing in just bra and pants, she began to remove her make-up.

For the past six months she had forcibly buried all the things he made her feel. Had fiercely pretended they didn't exist because nothing could ever come of them. But now... Now she didn't know what to do, or think. He'd probably been bored, she tried to tell herself, and if that had been the case then it was so unfair, because now her breasts ached, as did her loins. It had been a long time since she had snuggled up to a warm, male, naked body. Too long perhaps. But with Adam? Feeling hot again, she gave a little gasp as the bedroom door opened to admit him.

CHAPTER SIX

'YOU said—' she began in shock.

'Claris, I'm sorry. A child is missing,' he said urgently.

'What?'

'A child.'

'Child?' With an impatient little shake of her head, thrusting one hand through her tumbled hair, she apologised. 'Sorry, my mind's…'

'Not working,' he finished for her, 'yes, I know.' Carefully avoiding looking anywhere but at her face, he continued. 'They're asking for volunteers.'

'Right. Yes. Er…' Staring round her as though for inspiration, she asked, 'What do I need?'

'Clothes?' he asked drily.

Hastily staring down at herself, she blushed. 'Clothes, yes.' Grabbing the shorts she'd changed out of earlier, she struggled to put them on.

'I'll wait for you downstairs.'

'Yes.' As the door closed behind him she let all her breath out on an explosive sigh. Fool, she scolded herself. Idiot. For a moment there she had thought… Missing child, she reminded herself. Come on, pull yourself together. Dragging out a clean tee shirt from the drawer, she slipped it on, fastened her shorts, shoved her feet into sandals and ran.

And then she ran back. Best put on shoes; they'd probably be combing the fields. Dragging her sandals

off, she quickly rummaged in the bottom of the ward-
robe for her loafers, shoved her feet into them and
hurried out. She felt exhausted.

Adam was waiting in the hall, his mobile phone
and a torch in his hand, and he turned quickly at her
entrance.

'I've had a word with Lydia,' he said softly, 'and
she'll listen for the baby. Ready?'

'Yes.'

'Good girl. Come on.' Taking her hand, he led her
out of the side door and down to the lane. About a
dozen people were waiting for them beside an old
truck. Including Colonel Davenport.

A middle-aged man seemed to be in charge, and
he explained that the Colonel was to be co-ordinator.
'So, would all those with mobile phones please marry
up with those who haven't; leave your numbers with
the Colonel.' When that had been done, and pieces
of paper handed out with the Colonel's number on it,
they were given their areas to search. 'Groups of four,
I think. If nothing is found in your assigned areas,
make your way towards the river. The police are doing their own investigating.

'His name is Michael Dodd, and he's seven years
old. His mother put him to bed at his normal time,
but when she went to check on him when she herself
went to bed he'd gone. He's small for his age, fair
hair, dressed in blue shorts and a green tee shirt. It's
not thought he was taken, but has merely run away.'

A photograph was passed round, and as Claris
stared down at it she asked quietly, 'Is he from the
new estate?' When it was confirmed that he was, she
added with a rather sick feeling in her tummy, 'I think

I saw him yesterday, with some other boys.' Which was of absolutely no importance, she thought disgustedly, but had the horrible feeling that this could all be her fault. If it *was* one of the boys she'd seen, and if one of them *had* been responsible for her injury, then stopping the car as she had...

She hastily joined Adam, along with two others, and they headed towards the open land behind Grays Manor. Please be all right, she prayed to herself. Please, please be all right.

After endlessly calling, searching, four hours later, general worry had turned to fear. At least it wasn't cold, Claris tried to reassure herself, and he wouldn't be lying somewhere frozen. In fact, it was a hot, muggy night, and Claris wished she'd thought to bring a cold drink. Conversation between the searchers had petered out long ago. She thought they had probably all expected that the boy would be found quite quickly, but as several more hours passed, and the sky began to lighten, Claris began to feel more and more sick. The thought of a small boy, frightened and alone, was the stuff of nightmares. But pray God he *was* alone, and not... Hastily shutting off such negative thoughts, she accepted the long stick Adam handed her and began beating the long grasses beside the river. His mobile beeped suddenly, and she gave a startled yelp. Everyone within hearing distance halted and turned towards him.

Looking sombre, he answered it, and then he smiled. The most beautiful smile in the whole world, Claris thought at that moment. He spoke quickly, presumably to the Colonel, and then switched off.

'He's fine,' he explained to everyone in general.

'The Colonel doesn't know the details, just asked me to tell you he's been found safe and well, and to thank you all.'

Someone cheered, and everyone laughed in relief. As one, they turned back towards the road and the waiting truck. At last, slumped between Adam and a young man with long brown hair, Claris closed her eyes. Murmuring goodbye as each person was dropped off, she was nearly asleep when they reached Grays Manor. Adam helped her down, waved to the driver and escorted her inside.

'What time is it?' she asked without much interest and with a wide yawn.

'Half-five. Go and get some sleep.'

She grunted, yawned again, then smiled at him. Not so elegant now, but somehow still impressive. Hair sticky with burrs, chin beginning to show bristles, his shirt torn on one shoulder, he looked a wreck. An exciting, desirable wreck.

He touched gentle fingers to her face, and said softly, 'I'm glad you didn't query it.'

'Query what?' she asked with a small frown.

'Being dragged off to help with the search.'

Frown deepening, she asked, 'Why would I query it? I wouldn't have thought *anyone* would have refused to go.'

'Maybe. Go and get some sleep.'

'Yes.' She waited for a moment to see if he would kiss her, and when he didn't she turned disappointedly away. 'Goodnight.'

'Morning,' he corrected.

She merely smiled, climbed over the baby-gate, and walked heavily upstairs. She had wanted him to

kiss her. Just a gentle touch of his mouth on hers
would have been enough. But he hadn't. Perhaps he
was having second thoughts. Regretting his earlier behaviour.

Stripping off, too hot to get under the covers, she
lay on the bed and was instantly asleep.

She woke at noon, and groaned. She ached. They
must have walked *miles*. But the boy was safe, and
that, really, was all that mattered. Rolling over, she
stared at the ceiling and yawned. It was still hot.
Amazing—a whole week of hot weather. In *England*.
If this carried on, Adam would have to get a bigger
paddling pool.

Adam. What on earth was she going to do about
Adam? Or did she, in fact, need to do anything? She
probably shouldn't read anything into that little incident on the terrace, and it had been just an incident,
she tried to tell herself. Between girlfriends, he probably had been bored. A small diversion, that was all
she'd been. Thinking about it in the cold light of day,
she didn't suppose he wanted to have an affair with
her any more than she wanted one with him. It would
be foolish in the extreme to have a relationship with
someone she worked with, because when it ended—
as it would end—how could she continue working for
him? And yet the memory of his kiss brought a
warmth to her insides, a little flutter of excitement in
her chest. She just couldn't stop thinking about it.

Turning her head, she stared at her reflection in the
long mirror. Hardly an inspiring image, was it? Not
a face one could ever imagine Adam wanting to kiss.
And yet he *had* kissed her, had even said he'd like to
go to bed with her... Oh, will you just get up, Claris?

The man's a desperate flirt! Isn't he? She had no real evidence of that, just other people's opinions. The staff in the London office had talked about him quite a lot. But did they know him any better than she did? Adam only allowed you to see what he wanted you to see and nothing else. A few weeks ago she wouldn't have said he would be any good with a baby...

Impatient with herself, and determined to be sensible, as she was *always* sensible, she rolled to her feet and went to have her shower. Past caring about the butterfly tapes, she tilted her face to the cool water. She stood there for ages, just letting it wash over her, until, finally rousing herself, she soaped herself and shampooed last night's collected debris from her hair. Feeling fresher, and more or less awake, she put on a loose dress, dried her hair and went to start the day. If there was a flutter of anticipation in her chest, well, that was normal, wasn't it? Human.

Picking up the paper from the hall table, firmly telling herself that she wasn't in the least nervous about meeting Adam, she glanced at the headlines, registered the date, and gave a soft laugh. It was her birthday. How could she have forgotten it was her birthday?

Neither Lydia nor Adam would know because— well, she didn't suppose Adam had bothered to look at her CV since she'd handed it to him, certainly not to check on her date of birth. And there would be no cards or presents from her friends because she hadn't yet told them where she was living. Normally they would all go out for a meal, or a drink, but this year...

Well, birthdays were for children, she tried to assure herself.

Pushing into the kitchen, she grinned at the baby's noisy greeting and smiled at Lydia. 'Hello, it's good to see you back on your feet. Feeling better?'

'Much, headache's gone and the rash is fading. I expect you're hungry. What would you like to eat?'

'Oh, I don't know. Tea and toast would be fine. I didn't mean to sleep so late. Is Adam up?' she asked, rather too casually.

'I don't think he went to bed,' Lydia reproved. 'Or, if he did, he was up again at eight, because I heard him answer the phone—and then become very terse, not to say arctic to some poor unfortunate on the other end.'

'Oh, dear.'

'Quite. He said to tell you to take the day off.'

'Wow.'

'How was your date with the doctor?'

Claris pulled a face.

'That bad, huh?'

'No-o, but...'

'He wasn't for you,' Lydia stated as though she had known all along that he wouldn't be.

'No.' Accepting her toast and a cup of tea, she idly watched as Lydia tidied round. 'Has Adam mentioned anything about when the grandparents get out of hospital?'

'No, why?'

'Oh, no reason.' Finishing her breakfast, she got up to wash and dry her cup and plate.

'I can do that.'

'I know you can, but if I have the day off, I'm not entirely sure what to do with myself.'

'Go and sit in the garden. Read the paper, doze— answer the door,' she added, all in the same breath.

With a little laugh, Claris went to do so.

'OK, OK,' she said softly as the front doorbell pealed again. 'I'm coming.' Opening it, she stared in astonishment at the woman from the shop.

She thrust a small tin at Claris. 'Baking soda,' she announced, almost aggressively. 'I won't do it any more. If we lose the shop, we lose it, but I'm damned if I'm going to knuckle down to that woman any more.'

Staring at her, totally nonplussed, Claris hastily pulled herself together. 'Mrs Staple Smythe, do you mean?'

'Yes,' she agreed shortly. 'Like sheep, we are. Don't do this, don't do that! Well, I, for one, am going to do as I like. Anyone with eyes to see must know that you only work for him. You're no more his type than I am. And if he chooses to employ a secretary with a baby then that's *his* business! Not mine, not hers! You come in the shop any time you want!'

'Thank you,' Claris said weakly.

'And if *I* had a boss—which, thank God, I don't— then *I* wouldn't let her in to see him either!' With a brisk nod, she turned on her heel and walked away.

Slowly closing the front door, Claris stared at the tin in her hand. Dismissing everything else the woman had said, her mind latched onto one short sentence. *Anyone* could see? Yes, of course they could, she admitted sadly. It was what she knew herself.

What she had always known. She wasn't Adam's type. For a moment, one small moment, she'd been in danger of forgetting that, hadn't she? Because hope had... Hope? Yes, there had been hope. A very foolish hope, but hope nonetheless.

He thought her practical, and sensible, a little bizarre sometimes, but he wouldn't expect her to read anything into one small kiss, would he? No. He'd probably already forgotten it. And that was what she must do. She hadn't wanted him to kiss her. She hadn't expected that he ever would.

'Claris?'

Looking up, she saw the housekeeper standing in the kitchen doorway.

'I heard the front door close ages ago and wondered where you were. What's that?'

'Mmm? Oh...' With a little smile, unaware how wistful it was, she explained, 'Baking soda. Mrs Staple Smythe just lost a disciple.' Walking towards the housekeeper, face still thoughtful, she passed the tin over just as the front doorbell pealed again.

'Like Piccadilly Circus,' Lydia snorted.

'Yes. I'll get it.' Retracing her steps, Claris opened the front door again. A man and a woman in their late twenties, both fair-haired, and a little boy stood there.

'Mr and Mrs Dodd,' the man said almost gruffly. 'And Michael.'

'Oh, yes, goodness me, yes. Sorry, come in. How are you? A wretched night for you; you must both be exhausted.' Holding the door wide, she invited them in and took them along to the lounge. 'Can I get you some tea?'

'No, thanks all the same. We just came to say thank you, and—well, how *do* you say thank you? And apologise?'

'There's no need to do either,' she denied.

'He's not a bad boy, Miss Newman...'

'Of course he isn't,' she agreed gently. 'And it's Claris.'

'Harry and Lisa,' he responded.

Glancing at Michael, who looked mutinous and tearful all at the same time, Claris smiled. 'Please, won't you sit down?'

'It was an *accident*,' Lisa blurted earnestly as she stared at the fading splendour of Claris's eye. 'Not that we knew he had the dratted thing. Says he found it. Everybody out all night looking for him, and—' Breaking off, she suddenly began to cry.

'Oh, hey, come on, it's all right,' Claris soothed as she hurried over to pat her shoulder. 'Come on, come and sit down.' Leading her to the sofa, she sat her down, then seated herself beside her and took her hand. 'Why don't you show Michael the garden?' she said quietly to Mr Dodd.

He nodded, and led the boy out through the French doors.

'I'm sorry,' Lisa apologised. 'I'm not usually such a wet blanket. The police have been... We've never been in trouble! Never! Harry says he's just a kid, but...'

'He *is* just a kid,' Claris agreed, 'and it's probably all my fault,' she added guiltily. 'He ran away because of me, didn't he?'

Lisa nodded. 'When you stopped your car beside him the other day, he thought you knew. And apparently his friends kept telling him he'd be in trouble. Poor little lad seemed to think he'd go to prison... Oh, God, I'm sorry,' she apologised. 'You could have been blinded.'

'But wasn't.'

'No. I'm really sorry. He saw a police car last night, you see, after he'd gone to bed. He was looking out of his window and saw a police car. Thought it had come to arrest him.'

'So he got dressed and ran away?'

'Yes. Climbed out the window. He could have broken his fool neck! *Anything* could have happened to him. And so we just wanted to apologise and thank you. I've told him he has to say sorry.' She didn't look any too hopeful her young son was going to obey and Claris smiled as she remembered her own mutiny as a child, when forced to apologise to an adult.

'I'll go and have a word with him, shall I? I promise not to tell him off.'

'He deserves it.'

'But you've already done so, haven't you?' she asked gently. 'And his father, I expect.'

As though she hadn't heard, Lisa continued to stare at Claris, at her bruised eye, the butterfly tapes, and then said quietly, 'I didn't expect you to be like this.'

'How did you expect me to be?'

'Angry.'

'If Michael had fired the catapult at me deliberately I would have been, but he didn't, did he?'

'No. I've told him and told him to stay where I can see him, but—well, you know what boys are like. Apparently the only decent climbing tree is in the

village. They were firing at a loose stone on some-
body's wall. He didn't see you until it was too late.
Why aren't they speaking to you?' she blurted.

Claris gave a little blink, her mind on her own
guilt—because she *was* guilty in a way, wasn't she?
If she hadn't stopped her car... 'The villagers?' she
asked quietly. 'I don't honestly know. As far as I can
judge, it's because I upset Mrs Staple Smythe.'

Michael's mother pulled a face.

'You know her?'

'Know who she is. We don't move in the same
circles..'

'Think yourself lucky,' Claris retorted drily.

'Yes. Miss Newman?'

'Claris,' she corrected.

'Short for Clarissa?'

'Mmm. What a name to saddle a ginger-haired
child with.'

Lisa Dodd laughed, suddenly looked more relaxed.
'We were so nervous about coming. We went to
everyone else first to thank them. Then there was just
you and Mr Turmaine left, and it wasn't just thanking
you, but to explain about the catapult... We stood
outside your gate for ages... I mean, we didn't expect
the Colonel to come and ask Mr Turmaine to help
with the search!'

'Why?' Claris asked simply.

'Well, he's *important*, isn't he?'

'Of course he isn't, and even if he was, does that
mean he can't help look for a lost child?'

'No, of course not, it's just that...'

'Division of wealth makes it hard to—ask?'

'I suppose. We don't mix much with the village,

they don't talk to the likes of us—except the Colonel, of course. He's really nice. We had some trouble with vandalism last year... It seems to be a pet project of his. Anyway, we got to your gate, and Michael was beginning to panic...'

'And I thought feudalism went out with the Middle Ages,' Claris murmured, then smiled. 'I remember being seven,' she added simply. 'I was an absolute horror. So you see, I have no right to criticise anyone else. And it's all part of growing up, isn't it? Learning. And I expect the poor little chap is sitting out there in mortal terror waiting for the dreaded Miss Newman to come and tell him off. Let me go and put him out of his misery.'

Getting to her feet, she walked out into the garden. Michael and his father were sitting at the wrought-iron table, and as she came out, Harry got to his feet.

'Could I have a word with Michael?' she asked quietly.

He glanced at his son, then back to Claris, bit his lip, and walked inside to join his wife.

'Hello, Michael,' she greeted him softly.

His lips tightened, but he didn't look up.

Sliding out the chair next to him, she sat down. 'I haven't come to tell you off,' she reassured him. 'It was an accident, and accidents happen. I was frightened for the baby, you see, in the pram. If the stone had hit him, it could have been nasty. I know you won't do it again, because you're quite grown-up now, aren't you? And if you see anyone else doing it, or throwing stones—well, you'll know to tell them how dangerous it is, won't you? I didn't mean to frighten you into running away, so I'm sorry for that.

I just wanted to see how you were after your adventure.'

He gave her a little sideways glance, his lashes damp, and she smiled at him. 'Best always to own up when you've done something wrong, then it's over and you won't need to worry about getting into more trouble. 'Fess up, that's what I always say.'

''Fess up?' he whispered.

'Mmm. Say you're sorry, tell the truth, and then you won't need to be frightened and not know what to do. Sad to say, some people might shout at you, tell you off, but it will be over and no need to go on being unhappy and scared. And I expect you were scared, weren't you? All alone out in the dark. I would have been. Funny noises...'

He gave a vehement little jerk of his head. 'Ghosts.'

'Maybe,' she agreed. 'Who knows? Best just to tell someone when things go wrong. But now it's all over,' she added, even more gently, 'and you don't need to worry any more. Shall we go and find your mum and dad?' Getting to her feet, she waited for him to hop down.

'Miss?'

'Yes?'

'I'm sorry,' he said bravely.

'I know you are.'

'Does it hurt?'

'A bit, but I'm quite a brave soldier.'

He gave a tentative smile, and she smiled warmly back. Smoothing his tumbled hair off his forehead, she held out her hand. He put his own into it, and they went back into the lounge. Adam was standing just inside, talking to Harry Dodd. She half smiled at him, remembered he wasn't for her, and smiled at Lisa instead. 'All done,' she said brightly as the other woman got to her feet.

Harry and Adam shook hands and Claris escorted them back to the front door.

'You were right,' she said to Lisa as her husband and son walked ahead of them. 'He's a nice little boy.'

'Thank you. And if you ever need someone to talk to—I mean…'

Claris laughed. 'I might take you up on that.'

'I don't expect it's easy to talk to someone like Mr Turmaine,' she continued. 'He frightened me half to death. We all heard about his glamorous girlfriend,' she grinned. 'It's all round the village. A man like that—well, he could have his pick, couldn't he?'

'Yes.' Forcing a smile, Claris watched until they were out of sight. A man like that. Reluctant to face Adam, in case he should see something in her face that she didn't want him to see, she slowly closed the front door. Lydia was in the kitchen doorway, watching Nathan as he walked unsteadily behind his wheeled trolley. It couldn't be said that he was pushing it.

'Won't be long before he can walk without holding on,' she murmured. 'I've been trying to delay the process, so that his parents will be the ones to see his first steps…'

'But you can't change things, can you?' Any more than she could change herself into the glamour puss that everyone might think right for Adam. So don't be a fool, Claris. You never wanted to be anything other than what you are. And she had absolutely no desire for herself to be right for Adam, she told herself firmly. Or Adam to be right for her. So why were a few unguarded words from the shopkeeper, and now Lisa Dodd, still haunting her?

The phone rang in the study, but before she could get to it she heard Adam answer.

'No, I do not wish to expend further effort on trying to salvage it,' she heard him say coldly, and a few moments later, he argued astringently, 'I don't pay you for good ideas. I pay you to carry out my instructions. If you can't do that, which you obviously can't, then this conversation is pointless.' The receiver was quietly replaced, and Claris exchanged a glance with Lydia.

The housekeeper rolled her eyes and said quietly, 'I'm just making him some tea. I'll bring it out to the terrace.'

Claris nodded. Her eyes on Nathan, she wondered who Adam had been talking to. The only deals he was trying to put through at the moment, as far as she was aware, were the sale of some river-front land he owned and the takeover of a small engineering works.

When Adam didn't emerge, she walked to the study door and looked inside. He was sitting with his feet up on the desk, with a very blank expression on his face.

'Engineering works?' she asked quietly.

'Yes,' he agreed tersely. 'What happened to my tea?'

'Lydia's just making it. She said she'd put it on the terrace.'

He nodded. 'You didn't tell him off.'

'The catapult king? No.' Returning her attention to the baby, she smiled as he thumped to his bottom and turned the trolley over. An expression of wonderment on his face, he began revolving one of the wheels.

'Brrm, brrm,' Claris said, and Nathan turned to laugh at her.

'You're worse than he is,' Lydia observed as she passed carrying a tray.

'Never.' Bending, Claris righted the trolley, stood Nathan behind it and helped him towards the garden. Then she lifted both baby and trolley across the terrace and set them down on the grass, where he wouldn't hurt himself if he fell down.

She sat herself at the table whilst Lydia laid out the tea things, stiffening slightly when Adam walked out to join her. Should she mention the kiss? Tell him she didn't want him to do it any more? But supposing he didn't *want* to do it any more? Supposing he'd forgotten all about it?

'Claris,' he began quietly, but whatever he'd been about to say was destined to be left unsaid, because just at that moment Bernice strolled out, smiled at them both, and sat down.

'I heard what happened last night. You do have some fun down here. Nothing ever happens in Rye.'

'Not something I would want to happen anywhere,' Adam said in the quiet voice that could sometimes terrify.

'No, of course not,' she agreed hastily. 'Oh, goodness, he looks as though he's about to decimate the flowerbed.' Leaping to her feet, Bernice ran after the baby, picked him and the trolley up and set him down away from the flowers.

Nathan looked at her with the sort of look that usually left adults feeling wanting. Then the little boy plumped to his bottom and began crawling energetically towards the terrace. Reaching Adam, he hauled himself up and scrambled onto his lap. As Bernice joined them he turned big blue eyes on her, his face solemn.

'I'll fetch another cup,' Lydia said abruptly, and promptly disappeared inside.

Looking from one to the other, Bernice quipped, 'No happy bunnies today?'

Adam didn't answer, just kept his gaze on the baby and gently removed his hand when he reached for a cup. 'No,' he said softly.

Nathan looked at him, at Claris, stared at the cup, and blew a raspberry.

Bernice was the only one who laughed, then apologised. 'I shouldn't laugh, should I?' Turning to the housekeeper as she emerged with another cup, she thanked her.

'It's what I'm paid for,' she said shortly.

'Lydia...' Adam reproved.

The housekeeper sniffed and walked inside.

'Oh, dear,' Bernice murmured comically.

'We're all tired,' Claris explained, probably needlessly.

'Yes, of course you are. I shouldn't have come, should I? Shall I pour?'

Without waiting for an answer, she put milk in each cup, then poured the tea and handed it round.

The burden of conversation fell on Bernice. Not

that she seemed to find it a burden. After handing a finger biscuit to the baby, Claris took one for herself. Not that she really wanted it, but it was something to do whilst Bernice recounted amusing little anecdotes about her life in Rye.

Surreptitiously watching Adam, who looked profoundly uninterested in anything the other girl had to say, Claris wondered how angry he really was about the sabotaged deal. Very angry, she imagined. He'd spent a lot of time and effort setting it up. Well, no doubt he would tell her about it later. Glancing at the baby, she saw that he was falling asleep. He hadn't had his afternoon nap, which meant, she thought wryly, he would be asleep when he should be having his dinner, and then he would be late going to bed. Not that it mattered, she supposed. She was just about to make her excuses and take him up to his cot, when Adam interrupted Bernice's prattle.

'Claris gave the list to me,' he stated quietly.

Halted almost in mid-flow, Bernice gave him a puzzled glance. 'Sorry?'

'The list of your aunt's investments. Claris gave it to me.'

She gave him a bewildered smile. 'What list of my aunt's investments?'

He stared at her. So did Claris.

'You saw Claris in Rye the day before yesterday,' he stated softly.

'Yes,' she agreed slowly. 'She came for coffee.'

'And you asked her if she would kindly look over your aunt's investments because you were worried.'

She looked at Claris, an expression of bafflement

on her pretty face, and then at Adam. 'No. We had coffee and then Claris went home.'

'I see,' he murmured neutrally.

So did Claris. Or she was beginning to.

'You didn't admit to making anonymous phone calls?' he asked interestedly.

'Of course I didn't!' she denied with a laugh. 'Why on earth would I make anonymous phone calls? Look, I'm sorry, but we seem to have our wires crossed somewhere.'

'Mmm.'

'What does that mean?' she demanded. 'Either we have or we haven't! Certainly I can't think of any other reason why you would imagine I'd give Claris a list of my aunt's investments!'

'Claris,' he said.

'Claris?' she frowned. 'Claris *told* you that I gave her a list?' Turning her attention to Claris, she demanded with quite masterly bewilderment, 'Why? Why would you tell him that? I mean, they're nothing to *do* with me! I wouldn't even know what they *were*! Claris, you *can't* have told him that! I know Aunt Harriet can be a funny old stick at times, and that she probably put your back up at the party, but to invent a whole fabrication! No, I can't believe you did that. And no one would believe it anyway. Everyone knows I wouldn't do anything to upset her; she's been *enormously* kind to me. When my mother died of cancer last year it was Harriet who came to my rescue, Harriet who advised me what to do, took me off to stay with her after the funeral... Claris, you *can't* have said I gave you one of her personal papers.'

'But you did say that, didn't you, Claris?' Adam asked her softly.

'Yes,' she agreed.

He returned his attention to Bernice. 'You think Claris stole it?' he asked.

CHAPTER SEVEN

'WITHOUT your knowledge, of course,' he added smoothly.

'No!' Bernice denied. 'Claris wouldn't do anything like that!'

Claris gave a soft little shake of her head in agreement. Absolutely riveted, all thoughts of taking the baby up for his nap abandoned, she watched, waited, and remained silent.

'Oh, look, I feel terrible now,' Bernice murmured. 'I just don't know what to say! Claris?' she pleaded as she glanced at the other girl.

'No, no, no,' Claris denied with mock humour. 'Don't ask me.'

'But I didn't *give* you a list!'

'If you say so, Bernice,' she agreed almost amiably, but there was absolutely no humour in her wide grey eyes.

'But I *do* say so! I wouldn't *forget* something like that!'

'Of course you wouldn't.'

'Take the baby, would you, Claris?' Adam asked her quietly.

She turned to look at him, but could read nothing from his face. With a small, very unamused smile, she got slowly to her feet, carefully picked up Nathan and carried him inside. Careful not to wake him, she climbed awkwardly over the baby-gate and on up to his room. Laying him gently down, she drew the curtains, picked up the baby alarm, and walked out.

Well, well, well, she thought as she descended the stairs, who would have thought it? And *why* was she doing it? To make Claris look a fool? But she wouldn't, because Adam wouldn't believe it. Whatever else he might think of her, or not think of her, he wouldn't believe Bernice's little fabrication. Would he?

A moral problem, had she said? It was more than that, wasn't it? Stepping out onto the terrace, she barely had time to reach her chair when Lydia arrived.

'Mrs Staple Smythe,' she announced, in a voice of comical neutrality.

Perfect, Claris thought, all it needed now was Aunt Harriet. Not daring to look at Adam, she silently took her seat.

Mrs Staple Smythe nodded to Bernice, ignored Claris, and smiled at Adam. 'So sorry to interrupt,' she apologised regally, 'but I really do need to know if you will be coming tomorrow.'

Adam just looked at her.

'The meeting,' she prompted.

'What meeting would that be, Mrs Staple Smythe?'

'Why, the meeting I mentioned to Miss Newman when we met in Rye yesterday,' she lied without a blink.

He glanced at Claris, who shook her head.

'I really would have expected the courtesy of an answer,' she added.

'Would you?' he asked softly, and at his most dangerous. 'How odd that you should mention courtesy.'

She gave a bewildered smile. One that might even

have been borrowed from Bernice, Claris thought. 'I'm afraid I don't understand.'

'Don't you? But you should. You expect courtesy from others, but it's obviously not a concept you follow yourself. Hardly courteous to incite the whole village to ignore Miss Newman, is it? Goodbye, Mrs Staple Smythe; the gate is to your right. Close it behind you when you leave, won't you?'

She gave him a blank look. 'I'm afraid I don't know what you're talking about.'

'Another one. My, my.'

Her mouth tightened. 'I need to know if you will be attending any of our committee meetings,' she stated harshly.

'No,' he denied without elaboration.

'It would be in your own best interests,' she warned.

'Threats, Mrs Staple Smythe?' he asked even more softly. 'Be warned, I'm not a man to take them lightly. I make a very bad enemy. Something you would do well to remember. And if Miss Newman suffers any more unpleasantness,' he added dangerously, 'you will learn, to your cost, how much of an enemy I can be.'

'And you will learn the same!' she countered. Back rigid, she stalked away. She slammed the gate behind her.

'You too,' he said quietly to Bernice.

'Sorry?'

'You too.'

Looking from one to the other, she exclaimed, 'You want *me* to leave?'

'Didn't I make it clear?' he asked, almost pleasantly.

'But *why*? I haven't *done* anything!'

'Except lie. Answer that, would you, Claris?'

Getting to her feet, Claris walked inside to answer the phone.

'Hello? Oh, hello.' Listening for a moment, she said quietly, 'Yes, I'll tell him. Sounds promising, doesn't it?' Replacing the receiver, she returned to the terrace. And if neutrality could be said to be an expression, then Adam was wearing it. There was no sign of Bernice.

'That was this hospital,' she said quietly. 'Paul is asking to see you.'

He turned to look at her. 'He's *lucid*?'

'Apparently so.'

'Well, don't sound so damned casual about it.' Getting to his feet, he walked inside.

'I wasn't being casual,' she denied quietly. Not that he heard her. Not that she'd intended him to hear. And, as birthdays went, this was turning out to be a real lulu, wasn't it? Although, to be fair, she had received a tin of baking soda and an apology. Happy Birthday, Claris.

With a little grunt of not very amused laughter, she began clearing the table.

'And just what was that all about?' Lydia asked interestedly from behind her.

'Politics,' Claris said softly.

'The self-styled doyenne of Wentsham society is into politics?' Lydia asked derisively.

'No, into trying to destroy my credibility with Adam. Bernice seemed to be on the same mission.'

'He won't believe them over you.'

'No, but the even tenor of his days is being eroded, isn't it? And whose fault will that be, do you think?' With a deep sigh, she began shoving everything else onto the tray. Picking it up, she carried it through to the kitchen. Lydia meekly followed.

Everyone wanted her to look a fool, didn't they? And she was allowing it. Even Adam was at it. Stupid Claris, who walked through life with her eyes shut. She'd allowed Mrs Staple Smythe to circulate rumours about her, allowed Adam to kiss her. Had even responded—because it was what she had wanted. And everyone could see that she wasn't his type. Everyone. As she had always known. All these months she had pretended not to find him attractive. Had behaved as he wanted her to behave. Teased him, laughed at him, carefully trod the fine line between familiarity and subservience. But what other option had there been? None. Not if she'd wanted to remain working for him. Which she had.

'Claris?'

Turning, almost forgetting that the housekeeper was there, she gave her a lame smile.

'Are you all right?'

'Yes, I'm fine,' she murmured despondently. 'I forgot who I was, you see. Just for a while,' she added softly.

'I don't understand.'

'No, it's not important. I think I'll go for a drive.'

'It will soon be time for dinner.'

'I'll get something out. Adam's gone to the hospital; I don't know how long he'll be. Would you mind putting the baby to bed?'

'No. Go on, off you go.'

'Thanks.' Collecting her bag and car keys, she walked slowly round to the stables. Backing out, she drove down to the lane and turned left. She didn't know where she was going; it didn't much matter. One place was as good as another. Just somewhere quiet, where she could think things through.

She found a layby at the top of a hill, from where she could see the sea in the distance, and she parked there, staring almost blindly across the open countryside. She'd been in danger of making a fool of herself, hadn't she? But it was all right now. Now that she knew... The doctor had suspected, though, hadn't he? How many others had? Mrs Staple Smythe? Bernice? Lydia? Did the housekeeper suspect? She'd been very gentle with her just now, hadn't she? 'He should marry you,' she'd said.

Had everyone known but herself? And she'd been so damned philosophical about it all! About Arabella... She had always known she enjoyed his company, being with him. His fine mind, she thought with an expression of disgust. But how the hell could she not have known that she was falling in love with him? A veritable child would have known that. She was twenty-eight... Twenty-nine, she remembered. Today.

She couldn't stay with him, could she? Not if she was in love with him. But she couldn't go, either. Not until Nathan's parents were better. It wouldn't be fair. She didn't care about Bernice, or Mrs Staple Smythe; they weren't important. She didn't even know why they were doing it. It seemed so futile. Well, no, she did know why they were doing it. Bernice wanted to know about her aunt's investments, although it was a damned funny way of finding out, accusing Claris of masterminding it. And Mrs Staple Smythe was just a foolish woman who liked bossing everyone about. Who the hell cared?

The best thing, she decided, was to pretend she hadn't noticed Adam's interest... You can't not have *noticed* it, Claris. He kissed you, for goodness' sake! Pretend she thought he was joking, then, flirting. Yes, laugh it off; that was best. She could do that; she was very good at merry quips. Normally. Resting her head back, she stared at the distant sea. Have to do better than this, though, wouldn't she?

His fit of temper would help. She could pretend to be miffed. And she'd get over it. Of course she would.

He might have meant it... Claris, he didn't mean it. Adam Turmaine and herself? As lovers? It was ludicrous. It was as likely as—well, as likely as him and the lady from the shop. A car passed, stopped and reversed.

'You all right?' the man asked.

'Yes, thank you. Just—thinking.'

He gave her an odd look, a shrug, and drove off. Obviously not the best place to sit and daydream. No. Firing the engine, she drove on. She would have something to eat, a birthday drink, and then go home. She needed to check that Adam had everything for his board meeting, and then she could go to bed. He would be out all day tomorrow, and by Friday she would be better. A bit like Lydia's measles.

Taking the road back towards Rye, or Rye Foreign, she saw from the small signpost, she pulled into the forecourt of a pub. Tables and chairs were set out in the small front garden, and after ordering something to eat and a drink she went and sat there. She didn't much like dining on her own, and sitting here at least gave her something to watch. It might only be *traffic*, but it was something.

When the waiter brought her order, and mostly to distract her mind, she asked him curiously, 'Why is it called Rye Foreign?'

He laughed. 'Because we once belonged to Normandy. This whole area—the Manor of Rameslie, as it was known—was part of the Abbey of Fécamp. Don't know all the details,' he apologised. 'But when King John was forced to give Normandy to Philip of France, which included Rye, this small part was still owned by the Abbey and was therefore excluded. Rye Foreign.'

'So we should be speaking French? Or is it no longer owned by the Abbey?'

He gave her a comical look. 'To tell you the truth, I have no idea. I shouldn't think so. But I can tell you what a flackley is.'

'Now, why would I want to know what a flackley is?'

'Because it's interesting.'

'OK,' she agreed with a smile, 'what is it?'

'A small group of trees.'

'Thank you,' she said drily. 'I'm sure such information will one day come in very useful.'

'Of course it will. Enjoy your meal.'

Feeling a bit better for the silly conversation, she ate her cold meat and salad and then sat sipping her drink. That's a nice flackley, she could say to someone, somewhere. Or, I was thinking of having a flackley…what do you think? With a little chuckle, a small shake of her head for her absurdities, she didn't see the doctor drive past, nor see him pull into the car park. The first she knew of his presence was when he came to stand by her table.

'Hello, Claris,' he greeted her quietly. 'All by yourself?'

Looking up, she gave him a warm smile. 'Yes. Come and join me.'

'I wish I could, but I'm on my way to visit someone.' Resting his hands on the chair opposite, he added, 'But I'm glad I've seen you. I wanted to apologise for the other night.'

'Nothing to apologise for,' she denied.

'Yes, there is.' Looking down, as though gathering his thoughts, he continued quietly. 'The fact is, between you ringing me and us meeting for that drink, I met my ex-girlfriend, Maggie, again.'

'Ah,' she said softly.

'I hadn't seen her in over a year,' he explained. 'We were engaged to be married. Had a silly argument…'

'But you never forgot her.'

'No. She turned up the day we were meeting… I'm sorry, I should have told you then.'

'It doesn't matter,' she dismissed. 'Are you engaged again?'

'Working on it,' he smiled.

'I'm glad. Go on, go to your meeting.'

He glanced at his watch and nodded. 'Don't go getting any more stones thrown at you, will you?'

'I'll try not to.'

Leaning forward, he gently examined the cut on her

cheekbone. 'Coming along nicely,' he smiled. 'But leave the tapes on until Friday. How's Lydia?'

'Much better.'

'Good.' With a small wave, he began walking back to his car, then halted and turned back. 'I didn't lie to you, Claris. You are a lady I could have grown fond of...'

'If it hadn't been for Maggie,' she completed for him. 'Thank you.'

He nodded and continued on his way. The story of her life, she thought with a wry attempt at humour. Wouldn't even be able to console herself with the young doctor. And it would be dark soon. Time to go.

It was hot in the car, and she opened all the windows before driving off, then smiled as she passed a hotel. It was called the Flackley Ash, which was, of course, why the waiter had told her what it meant.

As she drove into the stables ten minutes later she saw Adam's car, and her sombre mood returned. She didn't want to see him, meet him, not just yet, but it couldn't be avoided, could it?

Lydia must have heard her car, because she was waiting in the hall when Claris let herself in.

'All right?' she asked quietly.

'Yes. Sorry about that. I just needed to be on my own for a while.'

'You don't need to explain,' Lydia said gently. 'Adam's in the lounge,' she informed her as she went back into the kitchen.

But she didn't want to see Adam. Walking quietly, she went into the study and began putting his papers into his briefcase.

'Hello,' he said quietly from behind her, and she stiffened slightly. 'I'm sorry for shouting at you earlier.'

'It doesn't matter,' she denied without turning.

'Yes, it does. We need to talk, Claris.'

'Not now, Adam. Please, not now. How was Paul?'

'On the mend. They think he'll make a full recovery.'

'That's good. I think that's everything,' she added as she snapped his briefcase shut.

'Are you all right?'

'Yes, of course.'

'How was the doctor?'

She did look at him then.

'I saw you,' he explained quietly, 'as I was driving home.'

'Oh, he was fine. Goodnight.' Without looking at him fully she walked past him, climbed the baby-gate, and slowly climbed the stairs. She knew he was watching her, could almost feel his eyes on her back, but she didn't turn. It was best this way. Really, it was best.

In the morning, she stayed in her room until she was sure he had gone, and then went down to the kitchen for her breakfast. She thought she behaved quite normally, speaking to Lydia and Nathan as she usually did. She spent the morning in the study, catching up on things; she re-read the prospectus from the broker about business angels, made a few notes, added a few queries of her own, and was conscious, as she never had been before, of time passing. Adam would probably be home about six. Maybe a bit before, depending on the traffic out of London.

Stop thinking about it. Determinedly picking up the phone, she spoke to Sara Davies. Mark was busy, she was told, but everything was fine. Replacing the receiver, she caught herself staring into space for endless minutes, and reached hastily for the newspapers. She read them all, cover to cover, marked out any items she thought might interest Adam, as she usually did, and left them on his desk.

After lunch, she took Nathan out to the garden to play in his paddling pool, and managed to finish the tape of his chatter; when Lydia came to collect him for his dinner, she went upstairs to change out of her wet skirt and top.

Taking extra care with her make-up and hair, because it would give her confidence to look her best, beginning to be more and more apprehensive as the time approached for Adam to come home, she scolded herself for a fool. He probably only wanted to talk to her about Bernice and Mrs Staple Smythe. He would be very casual, probably, his reprimands usually were, which was what made them so lethal. And then he might mention the kiss—just in passing, so to speak. Apologise, say it had been a mistake. Well, that would be all right; it was what she expected. Wanted. So why did she feel so nervous? She was never nervous. Irritated with herself, she threw her hairbrush on the bed and walked quickly downstairs.

Determined not to clock-watch, or listen for his car, she went out to sit on the terrace and stare at the garden. That lasted for all of five minutes. Jumping to her feet, even more annoyed with herself, she began touring the flowerbeds, and then, suddenly re-

membering the secret garden, she walked quickly to
the end gate and pushed it open. It had soothed her
before; perhaps it would now.

She should have brought a chair, then she could
have sat—and what? she wondered in disgust.
Communed with nature? Glancing at her watch, she
saw that it was five-fifty. Not long now. And then she
stiffened as she heard the gate open behind her.

'Lydia said she saw you heading this way,' Adam
said quietly.

Turning, she gave him a smile that she hoped was
the same as the ones she normally gave him, but
found that her eyes wouldn't quite meet his. 'How
did the meeting go?'

'Fine. Did you *arrange* to meet the doctor last
night?' he asked, almost casually.

Surprised by the question, she shook her head.
'Like you, he was passing, saw me, and came in to
have a word. You really ought to get the gardener to
do something about these weeds...'

'He was leaning over you.'

'He was checking the injury.'

'Are you seeing him again?'

'No, not socially anyway,' she denied as she swung
round the rickety pergola and got a splinter in her
palm for her stupidity. Staring at it, trying to pick it
out, she added foolishly, 'Maggie came back.'

'Maggie?'

'An old girlfriend of his. We ought to go back. It's
almost time for Nathan's bath.'

'Lydia is going to bath him. You didn't arrange to
meet him?'

'No, I went out on my own.'

'You aren't in love with him?'

'Of course I'm not in love with him!' she denied irritably. 'I barely know the man.'

'Then what's wrong?'

'Nothing,' she denied too quickly. 'What should be wrong? Do you know what a flackley is?'

'Yes, a group of trees. Will you marry me, Claris?'

Frozen to the spot, her attempts to pick out the splinter abandoned, she thought for a moment that she'd misheard. Slowly looking up, she stared at him. 'What?' she whispered.

'I asked if you would marry me.'

'Why?'

He gave a lop-sided smile. 'Because I think I went and fell in love with you,' he confessed, in parody of her own words about the baby.

'Don't be silly,' she said without thinking. 'You can't possibly be in love with me.' Not knowing what to do, for the first time in her life not knowing what to say, she asked desperately, 'Did you call in at the hospital?'

'No, I called in on Harriet.'

'Did you tell her...?'

'Yes.' With a sigh, a wry, self-mocking smile, he wondered if any other man ever met with such a luke-warm reception to their proposal. 'I discovered why Bernice behaved as she did,' he murmured. 'Harriet is a very tidy woman, precise,' he explained gently, and with a patience he didn't normally possess. 'She keeps all her private papers in a box in the bottom of the sideboard in the dining room. She noticed it had been moved, and that the papers inside had been dis-arranged. She asked Bernice about it...'

'And Bernice said that I was there,' Claris stated softly.

'Yes.'

'And in case Harriet came here to confront me she had to cover herself, pretend she knew nothing about it?'

'I imagine so, yes. She's also very deeply in debt.'

'Harriet?'

'No, Bernice. She badly needs some ready cash.'

'I see.' And she thought she did. 'She thought you might make her a suitable husband, didn't she? And if that failed…'

'There was always Harriet.'

'Yes. I'm sorry everyone keeps coming to bother you,' she said stiffly. 'It wasn't my intention.'

'I know,' he agreed as he advanced on her. 'You weren't even sure I believed you over them, were you?'

'No,' she mumbled nervously, and wasn't entirely sure whether she meant his question or his advance. 'The shopkeeper came yesterday,' she babbled frantically as he continued moving towards her.

'Did she?'

'Yes. She said that anyone with eyes to see would know that I was no more your type than she was.'

'Certainly *she* isn't,' he denied, ever more softly.

Breathing agitated, she stared at him like a trapped bird. 'You can't want to marry me, Adam.'

'Why can't I?'

'Because… It's because of Nathan, isn't it?' she offered quickly. 'Yes, that would be it. Because you suddenly decided that you'd like a baby like him and…'

'No.'

'No?'

'No.' Reaching her, he put his hands gently on her shoulders and drew her towards him. 'Don't look so frightened.'

'I'm not frightened,' she denied. 'I'm…'

'Astonished?' he mocked softly.

'Well, of course I'm astonished,' she exclaimed spiritedly. 'Anyone would be! I'm not pretty. Even my fondest admirer couldn't say that!'

'No,' he agreed.

Nonplussed, she stared up at him, and he gave a soft laugh.

'It isn't funny!'

'No, it isn't. I've never asked anyone to marry me before. You wouldn't believe how nervous I am.'

'No, I wouldn't!' she agreed staunchly. '*I'm* the one who's nervous! And why?' she demanded of herself.

'Because you're trying to reject me and I won't listen?'

'No! No. Oh, Adam,' she exclaimed despairingly, 'you can't want to marry me; it's ridiculous.'

'But I do.' Gently tucking one side of her hair behind her ear, he implored quietly, 'Believe it, Claris.'

Searching his eyes, his face, frightened without knowing why, she pleaded, 'How can I?'

'You didn't even suspect how I was beginning to feel?'

'No! I thought you were going to say kissing me was a mistake! That…'

'I never make those sort of mistakes,' he answered gently. 'You need time to think about it?'

'Yes!' she agreed gratefully.

'All right. Don't take too long.'

'Otherwise you might get bored and find someone else?'

'No, otherwise I'll be too old to father the family I want.'

'So it *is* about Nathan!' she exclaimed almost triumphantly.

'No,' he denied gently, 'it's about you. About a girl I can't, now, imagine living without.'

Not knowing what to say, she looked down, fiddled with his tie. 'I'm nothing special…'

'You're very special. I'm sorry for my foul mood yesterday,' he apologised.

'That's all right. You were annoyed about the engineering works, and about Mrs Staple Smythe turning up. Will you lose very much?'

'Enough. It doesn't matter. I'll recoup it somewhere else. You're not indifferent to me, Claris, are you?'

She shook her head.

'Attracted to me?'

She nodded. 'But I didn't know,' she lied hastily, just in case he might think she'd been angling for this. 'Not until you kissed me.'

'I know. Rather a dent to my ego,' he mocked himself.

'Yes,' she agreed without thinking.

He gave her a reproving little shake.

'Sorry.'

'That's all right; I dare say I deserved it. Do you think you might manage to look at me for more than one second at a time?'

Flicking her eyes up to his, and as quickly away

again, she gave a funny little sigh and leaned her forehead against his chest.

He put his arms round her, and, carefully feeling
his way, asked softly, 'Is it because of all the
Arabellas that have dotted my life?'

She gave a tiny shake of her head.

'They didn't mean anything, Claris. Not in my
heart. If any of them had walked away it wouldn't
have mattered.'

'But you would care if I did?' she asked carefully,
still not believing it.

'Yes. Why do you think yourself unlovable,
Claris?'

'I don't,' she denied.

'Only unloved by me?'

'Yes.'

'Why?'

'Because I'm not pretty, I suppose, or elegant. All
your girlfriends have been.'

'But I didn't fall in love with any of them.' Easing
her away slightly, he tilted up her chin, forced her to
look at him. 'One of the things I always liked about
you was your honesty. Be honest with me now. *Could*
you love me? No, don't look away.'

Could she? She thought she already did. It was believing that he loved her that was the trouble. Staring
into his eyes, beginning to feel decidedly weak and
helpless, she whispered, 'Yes, but…'

He put a finger across her lips and then replaced it
with his mouth. She was shaking slightly, but gradually, as he continued to kiss her, she began to relax
and kiss him back. For one awful, horrible moment
he had thought she was going to refuse him, and it

was then, perhaps more than at any other time, that he'd realised just how much he *did* love her, and how devastated he would have been if she'd refused. Was that how Arabella had felt? he wondered guiltily as he continued to savour the soft sweetness of Claris's mouth. This girl he'd fallen in love with had made him think, examine his motives. No one had ever done that before. And the feel of her, the warmth of her generous spirit, made him feel just a little bit humble. He wanted to shine in her eyes—and he didn't think he did.

Her fingers were in his hair, against his nape, and he gave a slight shiver at the sensation. Pulling her closer, feeling his own arousal, he immediately relaxed the pressure when he felt her stiffen. Lifting his mouth, however hard it was, he managed to smile. 'I know,' he teased softly, his voice slightly thick. 'You don't want to be rushed.'

'No,' she agreed gratefully. 'I don't mean to be…'

'I know you don't. Come on, I'll take you where it's safer.'

Catching her hand in his, he led her back towards the house, and she would never know, he thought with an inward smile, how very hard it was to be—casual. All his life he had taken what was freely given, and now, when he wanted something desperately, it wasn't being given at all. Not yet.

She made an excuse that she needed to go up to her room, and they parted at the staircase. Walking into the kitchen, he gave his housekeeper a rueful smile.

'She refused you?' Lydia asked worriedly.

'No, she needs time to think about it.'

'Then make sure you give it to her!' she warned. 'She's frightened.'

'You think I don't know that?'

'All her life,' Lydia continued, as though he hadn't spoken, 'I would guess she has relied only on herself, and now she's afraid to give her feelings into the care of another.'

'Especially when that other has a reputation for—ruthlessness.'

'Not to those you care about,' she defended quickly.

'Of which there are sadly few,' he replied softly, and with a rather mocking glint in his eyes.

'Hmph,' she scoffed. 'There aren't that many *worth* caring about. Don't start doubting your judgement, Adam, not at this late stage.'

He gave a soft laugh. 'I'm not. You like her, don't you?'

'As if you needed my approval! But, yes, I do. She was upset yesterday. Did you find out why?'

'It was my birthday,' Claris said from the doorway.

Turning, he smiled at her. 'It was a secret?'

Clearly embarrassed, she shook her head. 'No, of course not.'

'But you were feeling unloved?'

'I was feeling—confused. And I didn't see Mrs Staple Smythe in Rye the other day.'

He laughed. 'No, I don't suppose you did. I shall have to do something about that wretched woman. But not now. Now I'm going up to have a cold shower,' he teased, and gave a delighted laugh when she went pink. 'That's my girl. Go down fighting.'

'I don't intend to go down at all!'

Dropping a light kiss on her nose, he went out, and Claris turned to look at the housekeeper. 'He…'

'I know,' Lydia said gently. 'Don't let him rush you. He's a good man, Claris.'

'I know,' she agreed. 'Did you know? I mean, suspect? Only, you said…'

'He should marry you? Yes. It took him a while to figure it out, but, yes, I always suspected you would be the one for him.'

'But *why*?' she asked in genuine bewilderment.

'I don't know,' Lydia denied slowly. 'Perhaps because you aren't intimidated by him, don't covet his wealth. You treat him like a human being. Not many people do, you know.'

'I know, but that's no reason to fall in *love* with me! It doesn't make any sense, Lydia!'

'When did love ever make sense?' Lydia asked her. 'Why are *you* in love with him?' she parried.

Claris gave her a sharp glance, and then a rueful smile. 'I don't know. I didn't even know I *was* falling in love with him.'

Walking out and into the dining room, still bewildered, she rather expected that their meal together would be awkward, but it wasn't. He made no further personal comments, just talked lightly about the board meeting, about the baby, but towards the end of the meal she began to feel nervous again.

'Are you going to the hospital this evening?' she broke in quickly.

'Is that what you would like?' he asked gently. 'For me to make myself scarce?'

Not answering directly, she said, 'I finished the tape.'

'Then I'll take it with me.'

She nodded. Finishing her coffee, she went to get it. Handing it to him, she said softly, 'Drive safely.'

'I will. Don't worry about it too much, Claris, just remember that I love you.'

She swallowed, nodded, and gave him a small smile. 'I'll have an early night, I think.'

'All right.' Bending his head, he gave her a warm kiss, then quickly left.

She spent the evening watching television, and taking in none of it. His words just kept repeating over and over in her head—he was in love with her. Unbelievable as it sounded, he wanted to marry her. And it scared her.

Almost afraid that she would still be up when he returned, she went to bed at nine-thirty—and couldn't sleep. *Why* was she so afraid? she wondered. Why couldn't she believe? She had always believed in herself. Always. Was it the emotion she was afraid of? Rejection? It was true she always needed to be in control. Whether it be friendship, or love, she only ever gave a small portion of herself. Never had she allowed herself to love fully. No, she thought miserably, she'd never *learned* how to love fully. No parents to teach by example, only strangers who'd done their best. And if she now allowed fear to override her feelings, she would never know what it was like to be loved, would she? And he surely wouldn't have told her he loved her if he didn't.

She heard him come home and her heart jerked in panic. Heard him come upstairs and go into his room.

She should go and talk to him. Clarify it to herself and to him. Discuss it, be rational, honest.

Before she could change her mind, feeling almost ill and shaky, she got up, slipped on her robe, walked determinedly along to his room and tapped on his door. *Made* herself stand there and wait.

'Come in.'

Taking a deep breath, emptying her mind of any thoughts at all, she pushed open the door. 'I need reassurance,' she said in a rush.

'Then come in and let me give it to you,' he answered softly.

CHAPTER EIGHT

CLOSING the door behind her, and desperately needing the support, she leaned back against it. 'I couldn't sleep,' she blurted, and then stated equally quickly. 'I shouldn't have come. I'll go.' Half turning, she halted when he quietly called her name.

'Come here,' he ordered softly.

Swallowing hard, fighting not to chicken out, and on legs that felt like rubber, she walked unsteadily across to his bed. The curtains were undrawn, so she could see his faint outline as he sat propped up against the headboard, the duvet covering him to the waist. See the small movement he made as he invitingly patted the quilt.

Perching on the edge of the bed, shaking so hard she thought he must feel it, she stared at her knees. I can't do this, she thought. I can't. Almost leaping to her feet, she was unprepared for his quick lunge to prevent her. 'I can't,' she whispered.

'Then tell me why,' he persuaded gently.

Sinking back down to the mattress, more because her legs wouldn't support her than for any reasons of wanting to stay, she whispered miserably, 'Because I'm a coward. And I *ache*. Oh, Adam, you have no idea how I ache.'

Afraid to pull her towards him, afraid of frightening her, still keeping hold of her arm, he shuffled nearer. 'I ache too,' he told her softly.

'Do you?'

'Yes. Come here.'

Almost overwhelmed by the nervous palpitations in her chest she risked a look at him, and then exclaimed almost in despair, 'You aren't *meant* for me, Adam!'

'And you'd ruin my life because you think you aren't good enough for me?'

'I *am* good enough for you!' she retorted. 'It's just…'

'You're afraid I might hurt you?'

'No,' she denied, 'but whenever I imagined getting married, it was never to someone like you. It seems so—ludicrous. You make me feel…'

'Tell me,' he persuaded softly. 'How do I make you feel, Claris?'

Twisting her fingers together, she explained bravely, 'Ever since I…' She began again, with a determination that almost broke his heart. 'Ever since I first met you, I've been fighting an attraction for you, laughing at myself, scoffing, because you weren't for me. I *knew* that, Adam, and I could deal with it. I thought perhaps you would never marry, or, if you did, it would be to someone I liked, and I could deal with that too. I liked you, liked working for you… And then I discovered that what I felt for you was more than liking. Ever since you kissed me on the terrace, in fact, my emotions have been seesawing about like—well, like a seesaw. And when the lady from the shop and then Lisa Dodds both said practically the same thing—that anyone could see that I wasn't your type—it was almost a relief, because I *knew* that.'

'And then I asked you to marry me.'

'Yes. It never even occurred to me that you could feel—what you say you feel, and so I didn't know what to do. And tonight, lying in bed, so hot, so—aching, thinking and thinking about it, wanting something that I never thought could be mine, I knew I had to come and talk to you about it. Because if I didn't, if I threw it all away...' Turning abruptly to face him, her eyes wide and distressed, she exclaimed, 'I want what you're offering. I want it so *much*—but I don't know how to love. I've never admitted that before, not to myself, not to anyone—didn't know I needed to. But going over and over it in my mind, I think I would have chosen someone safe. You aren't safe, Adam,' she added, with a seriousness that made him want to hold her and never let her go.

'You think I might one day come to my senses and reject you?' he asked carefully. 'Because you were rejected as a baby?'

'I don't know,' she denied worriedly.

'But you think someone safe might not do that?'

She gave a helpless shake of her head. 'It's not a conscious thing. I mean, I never even thought about it until tonight. But there has to be a reason why I back off from certain relationships, mustn't there?'

'You've backed off before?'

'Yes. Not like this, because I've never felt like this, but thinking back, yes. If it started to get serious, emotional, I'd back off. I told myself that it was because I liked my own space, that it was claustrophobic...'

'You don't have any close friends?'

'Yes, but I don't tell them anything—I didn't realise I didn't...'

'But with all this soul-searching you've been doing
tonight you've discovered a lot about yourself?'

'Yes. At least, I *think* I've discovered it.'

'Tell me about them,' he persuaded. 'Come and sit
down properly—me under the duvet, you on top...'

She gave a weak chuckle. 'I don't know why you
aren't on top. You must be roasting in there.'

'I am, but I don't have anything on, and when you
knocked on the door...'

'You scrambled underneath?'

'Mmm.'

'You were embarrassed?'

'No,' he denied. 'I thought you might be. Come
on, I'm getting a crick in my back leaning over like
this.'

'All right.' Turning, she sat on the bed beside him
and leaned back against the headboard. She carefully
kept her hands in her lap, avoided looking anywhere
near his naked chest. But it was hard not to touch
him, to nestle close. It was something she thought she
wanted more than anything else in the world.
Constant denial seemed to have made her feelings
fiercer.

'Tell me about your friends,' he persuaded softly.
'What are their names?'

'Oh, Sally Jenkins—she lives not far from me in
Edinburgh Road. Mike and Janey Cooper, the
Dawson twins—we go out together sometimes.
Parties...'

'Birthdays?'

With a small smile, she nodded. 'Yes, birthdays.'

Heart still beating over-fast, unbearably conscious of his nakedness, she had to clench her fingers tight together to stop from touching him. And then wondered what he would do if she *did* touch him. Voluntarily. He didn't seem tense, not like she was, and his breathing seemed quite regular. 'Adam?'

'Mmm?'

'If...' Turning her head, she found his face a great deal closer than she'd expected—and forgot what she'd been going to say. Staring into his shadowy eyes, scant inches from her own, she swallowed hard and moved her gaze to his mouth. So close, so unbearably close. All she would have to do was lean just slightly forward and her mouth would touch his.

He didn't dare move. He knew that if he touched her, instigated anything, she would leap away like a startled deer. And so he sat, breathing almost suspended, and waited.

'Oh, to hell with it,' she muttered, and kissed him. Not gently, not restrainedly, but with a passion that had been filling her up, building and building to explosive proportions ever since she'd gone to bed. Coming into his room had curbed it for a while, as nervousness had taken over, but now, with him so close, so naked, all restraint fled. She wanted this, and she was suddenly damned if all her cock-eyed reasoning was going to prevent it. If he didn't want her passion, then he was going to have to say so.

Mouth clamped to his, hands holding his face, she turned, scrambled backwards and dragged him sideways so that she could reach him properly. He shifted to accommodate her, held her and kissed her back with as much restraint as he could currently muster.

Just as suddenly she released him, and stared down at him. 'Is the restraint for your benefit, or mine?' she demanded tartly.

He stared at her for a moment in silence, and then he laughed, a warm, intimate chuckle that made the bed shake. 'Oh, Claris, how I adore you. For yours, of course. You don't want restraint?'

'No, I want to feel your—love. It has to be urgent and inescapable and overwhelming. Make me believe, Adam,' she urged quietly. 'Show me how much it matters to you.'

He searched her face, her ordinary and yet so appealing face, the wide grey eyes, the beautiful mouth, the sheer earnestness of her at this moment, the tumbled hair that she insisted was ginger and he thought of as new-minted copper. He gently turned her, kicked aside the quilt, and lay above her. Eyes still on hers, and with a hand that shook slightly, he carefully pushed the tangled curls back from her damaged cheek. 'I love you, Claris,' he said huskily. 'And for the first time in my life I'm afraid. Because it matters. Dear God,' he breathed, 'how it matters. And whatever happens now, whatever I do or don't do, the sombre fact remains that if I get it wrong, my happiness, my whole future, could be in jeopardy.' Moving his eyes to her mouth, he slowly narrowed the distance between them and began to kiss her as he had wanted to kiss her for what felt like a lifetime. One hand still in her hair, he let the other roam. He needed the feel of her, the taste, the warmth. With incredibly gentle fingers he pushed the neck of her robe aside. She wasn't wearing a nightdress, and he tried to regulate the tension in himself as his fingers found her breast. Her breathing was erratic, jerky, and her warmth was undermining all his good intentions. He wanted to bury himself in her and stay there for ever.

He dragged her belt free and tossed it to the floor, trailed his fingers down over her flat stomach to the tangle of hair that protected her womanhood—and couldn't stop shaking. He'd made love to many women, but he didn't think anything had ever prepared him for this.

She was kissing him back with a hunger that sent his own spinning into overdrive, holding him, touching his back with feverish little movements that severely threatened his control. She might have said urgent and overwhelming, but he hadn't been quite sure that she'd meant it.

Unable to wait, unable to contain all the feelings rioting inside, she pushed him onto his back, knowing that he allowed her to do so, and lay across him, her full breasts touching his chest, her thigh against his. Burying her mouth against him, she began to explore his exquisite body. Waist, hip, stomach, manhood. He jerked, and she felt a savage satisfaction. Mouse, had he once thought her? No, she was no mouse. As his hands shaped her back, her buttocks, with an urgency that thrilled her, part of her couldn't believe it was herself here, touching, inviting him to touch her most intimate places, needing to cover every inch of him with her hands, her mouth.

There was only the sound of their laboured breathing, her soft moans and exclamations, the slither of the duvet finally hitting the floor. Acquiescent no more, gentle no more, he turned her onto her back, and when a thousand compulsive kisses had been exchanged, when energy and tension had been driven out, and breathing was so erratic it threatened life, she clung to him, exhausted and shaking.

He held her just as tightly, his eyes closed, his heart labouring.

It took a long time for them both to regain the energy to move, and it was he who stirred first. Slowly lifting his head, opening his eyes, he stared down at her. Her eyes were still closed, her mouth slightly open as she pulled air into her depleted lungs, and then her lashes fluttered and she looked at him.

'Now do you believe we were made for each other?' he asked on a soft breath of sound.

'Yes,' she agreed huskily, and had to clear her throat in order to continue. 'I didn't know I could behave like that.'

He gave a quirky smile. 'I think I suspected. Hoped, anyway. And so now you will have to marry me, make an honest man of me.'

'Will I?'

'Yes. I might be pregnant.'

She gave that little choke of laughter that so captivated him, and then her smile widened, took up nearly the whole of her face, crinkled the butterfly tapes on her cheek. Tracing his mouth with a finger that shook, she mused softly, 'And I don't suppose Wentsham is ready for an unmarried father any more than it was able to cope with an unmarried mother.'

'No.'

'And Mrs Staple Smythe will die of shock. Almost worth it just for that.'

'Almost?'

Lowering her lashes, moving her finger to his throat, she murmured quietly, 'I still don't understand how I couldn't have known. You must think me very stupid.'

'No, I think you were very afraid to trust your emotions to someone else. But you can trust me, Claris.'

'I know. I *do* know,' she repeated as she raised her eyes again. And then she smiled. 'Still want to marry me?'

'More than anything.'

'People will be astonished.'

'And you think I will care?'

'No,' she chuckled, 'but I think it will take me a little time to adjust to the fact that you are no longer only my boss. That I can kiss you when I want to. Hold you.' With a funny little sigh, she wound both arms round his neck. 'We fit very nicely together, don't we?'

'Yes.'

'And you do realise that I won't be able to leave you alone, don't you?'

'It's my fervent hope.'

She smiled again, began to stroke the nape of his neck. 'We could get a lock put on the study door...'

His eyes gleamed.

'Just in case, you know, I suddenly get taken with passion. The way you sit sometimes, with your feet up the desk, might invite—all sorts of things.'

'I shall sit like it all the time,' he promised. 'Say yes.'

Eyes darkening, her body melting, she stared at his

mouth. 'Yes,' she whispered as her lips touched urgently against his.

'What about Nathan?'

'Get him back by five. But don't let Claris come in! No, on second thoughts, toot your horn and I'll come out and collect him, then you can just drive off again.'

Adam gave his housekeeper a dry glance.

'You could take her to the hospital, although thankfully, thankfully, that isn't something you'll have to do for much longer. After all the worry and the anguish, to finally know that Paul and Jenny are both going to make a full recovery...'

'Yes,' he agreed, 'and isn't it just a fine way to thank you for all you've done by now leaving you to feed and bath Nathan, get the food ready...? How on earth will you manage it all? You should have let me get caterers in...'

'And have a lot of strangers messing up my kitchen? No, thank you, and women have been taking care of children and organising parties for generations. I've put his lunch and dinner in the bag; any restaurant will heat them up for you. They are all coming?'

'Yes, I've booked them into the local hotel.'

She sniffed. 'I still don't know how you managed to get her to tell you who her friends were, *and* where they lived.'

'I only needed one—a Miss Sally Jenkins. She contacted the others.'

'Claris might not like surprise parties.'

'She doesn't have a choice,' he said softly. 'If she

can't tell people when her birthday is, she will have to put up with the consequences. Did you manage to get the candles for the garden?'

'I did—and, yes, I will put them out in the flowerbeds and round the terrace. Yes, I got the food. Yes, I invited the couple from the shop, and the Dodds, and Colonel Davenport. And your aunt Harriet.'

He pulled a face.

'You can't *not* invite her—all right, all right, *you* could, but *I* won't. Claris will expect it.'

'And what Claris expects, Claris must have?' he asked softly.

'On this occasion, yes.'

They both heard footsteps in the hall, and Lydia hissed hastily, 'And don't you dare bring her back before eight!'

He merely smiled.

'Well, I'm ready, as instructed,' Claris announced with a rather bewildered smile. 'Where are we going?'

'To get your engagement ring, of course.'

'Adam, I don't *need* an engagement ring! I mean, nowadays...'

'I need you to have one,' he said softly, and with finality. 'Grab the bag, will you?' Plucking Nathan out of his highchair, he hoisted him into his arms. 'We'll see you later,' he tossed to Lydia over his shoulder.

As instructed, he returned her at eight o'clock. Hustling her up to her room, he briefly kissed her, opened her door and ushered her inside. 'You have half an hour to shower and change. We'll eat on the terrace. I'll call for you,' he added with a dry smile. 'As a gentleman should.'

Resisting all attempts to get her into her room, she grabbed the doorhandle. 'Adam, what is going on?'

'Indulge me,' he said softly. 'I'm trying to be romantic.'

Searching his face, not entirely sure he was telling the truth, she finally nodded and went inside. He was behaving very strangely, and why they'd had to drive to London for her engagement ring she had no idea. Glancing down at the large diamond cluster, she gave a bewildered smile. It must have cost the earth. Carefully taking it off before going to shower and change, she laid it almost reverently on the dressing table. She was going to be terrified of losing it. She would much rather have had something simple. No, she wouldn't, she thought with a little grin, any more than she would have preferred a cheap dress to the one he'd insisted on buying her in Harrods.

Taking it out of its box, she laid it on the bed. Deceptively simple in chiffon crêpe, it looked nothing off, but on—well, on, that was another story. But to waste it on dinner on the *terrace*? Well, that was what he'd said. Wear the new dress.

She still couldn't quite believe it. That he could love her. She was in no doubt that she loved him, but that *he* should love *her*? And then she remembered their lovemaking, and felt warmth suffuse her. No reluctance on his part there. Or on hers.

When she was finally ready, she stared at herself for a very long time in the cheval mirror. She looked most unlike her usual self. Elegant, and sort of—special. Apart from pearl ear-studs and her engagement ring, she wore no other jewellery; the dress didn't need it. The halter neck set off her tan—and exposed rather a lot of flesh, she thought dubiously, but it did look nice with her hair up, high heels and a spray of expensive perfume. She wondered a trifle doubtfully whether Adam would expect her to always look like this. Always elegantly turned out, always immaculate. Not that she was normally a scruff, but... The little tap on the door made her jump.

'Come in.' Still staring at herself in the mirror, she watched his reflection approach. *He* was dressed casually, in a short-sleeved shirt and grey trousers, but the warm approval in his eyes made her heart leap.

'You look lovely,' he said softly.

'Thank you,' she whispered. 'You don't think it's a little bit too elegant for dining at home?'

'No.' Reaching her, he bent his head to drop a light kiss on her exposed neck, trail one finger seductively down her naked back. 'Ready?'

She nodded and turned to face him. 'Did I say thank you?'

'You did,' he reassured her with a small smile as he caught her hand in his. 'Come on, I'm hungry.'

Feeling decidedly strange and unreal, she walked down the stairs with him. The baby-gate had actually been *opened* and she gave him a wry glance.

'Can't have you climbing over it in your finery, can we?' Tugging her towards the kitchen, he tapped on the door, and then led her along to the lounge. The curtains were drawn, although the windows behind them must be open because they were fluttering in the breeze.

'Why are they...?' she began, but he merely

smiled, positioned her in front of them, and opened the curtains—and what sounded like a hundred voices yelled, *'Surprise!'*

Totally and utterly astonished, she just stood there. All her friends were here, and Harry and Lisa Dodd, the couple from the shop, Colonel Davenport, even Aunt Harriet! Tables and chairs dotted the lawn, candles flickered in the flowerbeds and on the terrace, and a long table laden down with food stood to one side. Overwhelmed, she just stared.

'Happy Birthday,' Adam said softly. 'And you're not to cry!'

'But you *hate* parties!'

'I shall manfully try to overcome my dislike,' he drawled. 'Go and greet your guests.'

Turning to look at him, at the love and amusement in his dark eyes, she felt her own mist with tears. 'I love you,' she whispered. 'Oh, Adam, how I love you.' She gave him a fierce hug, took a deep breath, and stepped out and onto the terrace.

'I love you too,' he responded softly, before stepping out behind her.

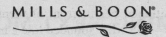

MILLS & BOON®

Makes
any time
special

Enjoy a romantic novel from
Mills & Boon®

Presents...™ *Enchanted*™ TEMPTATION.

Historical Romance™ **MEDICAL**
ROMANCE®

COMING NEXT MONTH

MILLS & BOON®

Enchanted™

THE DRIFTER'S GIFT by Lauryn Chandler

When Sam McClean stayed with Danielle for Christmas, he found it all too easy to become involved with her and her son. Now he had to find a way to make them his family for real!

BRIDE 2000 by Trisha David

Bryn Jasper had sabotaged Sophie's minister grandfather's ambition to marry his 2000th couple on the first day of the year 2000. Sophie wanted justice. But she never expected that she'd become Bryn's own millennium bride!

THE PARENT TEST by Elizabeth Duke

Cam Raeburn and Roxy both want custody of orphaned baby Emma—and Cam's solution is marriage! Roxy has one month to make up her mind—or the custody battle begins!

RESOLUTION: MARRIAGE by Patricia Knoll

(Marriage Ties)

Mary Jane is confused: Garrett is acting as if he never wrote to end their relationship all those years ago. And now he wants her back! She is tempted, but has to keep her distance. At least until she is ready to share her secret…

Available from 3rd December 1999

Available at most branches of WH Smith, Tesco, Martins, Borders, Easons, Volume One/James Thin and most good paperback bookshops

COMING NEXT MONTH

MILLS & BOON®

Enchanted™

LONG-LOST BRIDE by Day Leclaire

(Fairytale Weddings)

Nine years after Shayne was forced to end her marriage to Chaz, she meets him again at a masked ball where they have to marry by midnight. But can Chaz ever truly forgive her for the past?

THE BACHELOR'S BARGAIN by Jessica Steele

When Yanice's gorgeous boss, Thomson Wakefield, pops the question from his hospital bed, she has to ask herself if she can trust the proposal of a man under heavy sedation…

CLAIMING HIS CHILD by Margaret Way

Nick intended to make Suzannah pay for betraying their love seven years ago, even though his feelings still ran deep for her. Then he looked into the eyes of Suzannah's young daughter and recognised his own child…

DESERT HONEYMOON by Anne Weale

When Dr Alexander Strathallen confessed he wanted an heir and suggested a marriage of convenience only, Nicole agreed. But on her wedding night in the heat of the desert she found herself wanting more…

Available from 3rd December 1999

Available at most branches of WH Smith, Tesco, Martins,
Borders, Easons, Volume One/James Thin
and most good paperback bookshops

Celebrate the Millennium with your favourite romance authors. With so many to choose from, there's a Millennium story for everyone!

Presents...™

Morgan's Child
Anne Mather
On sale 3rd December 1999

Enchanted™

Bride 2000
Trisha David
On sale 3rd December 1999

TEMPTATION®

Once a Hero
Kate Hoffmann
On sale 3rd December 1999

Always a Hero
Kate Hoffmann
On sale 7th January 2000

MEDICAL ROMANCE™

Perfect Timing
Alison Roberts
On sale 3rd December 1999

MILLS & BOON®
Makes any time special™

MILLS & BOON®

MISTLETOE *Magic*

Three favourite Enchanted™ authors bring you romance at Christmas.

Three stories in one volume:

A Christmas Romance
BETTY NEELS

Outback Christmas
MARGARET WAY

Sarah's First Christmas
REBECCA WINTERS

Published 19th November 1999

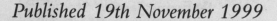

MILLS & BOON®

Makes any time special™

By Request

Bestselling themed romances brought back to you by popular demand

Each month By Request brings you three full-length novels in one beautiful volume featuring the best of the best.

So if you missed a favourite Romance the first time around, here is your chance to relive the magic from some of our most popular authors.

Look out for

Mothers-To-Be

in November 1999

featuring Jessica Steele, Catherine George and Helen Brooks

FREE!
4 Books
and a surprise gift!

We would like to take this opportunity to thank you for reading this Mills & Boon® book by offering you the chance to take FOUR more specially selected titles from the Enchanted™ series absolutely FREE! We're also making this offer to introduce you to the benefits of the Reader Service™—

    ★ FREE home delivery
    ★ FREE gifts and competitions
    ★ FREE monthly Newsletter
    ★ Books available before they're in the shops
    ★ Exclusive Reader Service discounts

Accepting these FREE books and gift places you under no obligation to buy; you may cancel at any time, even after receiving your free shipment. Simply complete your details below and return the entire page to the address below. **You don't even need a stamp!**

YES! Please send me 4 free Enchanted books and a surprise gift. I understand that unless you hear from me, I will receive 6 superb new titles every month for just £2.40 each, postage and packing free. I am under no obligation to purchase any books and may cancel my subscription at any time. The free books and gift will be mine to keep in any case.

N9EB

Ms/Mrs/Miss/Mr ....Initials...
                                                  BLOCK CAPITALS PLEASE

Surname...

Address..

....

....Postcode ....

Send this whole page to:
UK: The Reader Service, FREEPOST CN81, Croydon, CR9 3WZ
EIRE: The Reader Service, PO Box 4546, Kilcock, County Kildare (stamp required)

Offer not valid to current Reader Service subscribers to this series. We reserve the right to refuse an application and applicants must be aged 18 years or over. Only one application per household. Terms and prices subject to change without notice. Offer expires 31st May 2000. As a result of this application, you may receive further offers from Harlequin Mills & Boon Limited and other carefully selected companies. If you would prefer not to share in this opportunity please write to The Data Manager at the address above.

Mills & Boon is a registered trademark owned by Harlequin Mills & Boon Limited.
Enchanted is being used as a trademark.